THE SOLDIER

AND THE

CAMELLIA

Be worthy
They paid the ultimate price
The quiet unsung heroes
Their graves we may never find
Their sacrifices we may never know
For people they would never know
Let their lives not be forgotten
Honor them by honoring others
Live a life that they gave theirs for
Be worthy of them

PROLOGUE

Images just below her consciousness would be triggered by the slightest thing. A noise, a smell, or a sound, and the memories would surface. A loud noise and she would hear the bombs again, a fire in the fireplace and she would see the flames of the burning train, someone yelling and she would hear the screams from that night, feel the fear and the panic and the urgency of the victims and the rescuers. Sometimes there would be no trigger at all. The memory would rise up of its own as if it forced her to remember. Even though it was three years ago, she knew she would never be able to forget.

It was the arrival of the men that brought the memories back this time. When they first came to her house, she had an ominous feeling of dread. She decided to listen in on the conversations they had with her parents to hear what they wanted. When she heard them asking about the day of the bombings, her apprehension increased. The men wanted to know every detail about the bombing of the train. As her parents told everything they could remember to the men, Dominique relived the event. Over the next few weeks as the men kept coming back for more information, she began having the bad dreams again. She would wake up gasping for breath and crying as the memory of the war surfaced. She hated that time, when every day brought fear, when she would hear the sirens and everyone had to go into the cellar, and the nights that they had to spend in darkness and silence. She just knew then that they were all going to die. It seemed as if it would never end, that life was going to be like that forever. But finally the day came when it was announced that the war was over. Still it took a long time to actually believe it. Life was still not back to what it was before the war, if it would ever be.

She hated it every time the men came back. They questioned everyone that was involved with the event, all her family and the neighbors. The men wanted to know every detail, names, dates, and what happened to the people that they rescued and what they did with the bodies of the deceased. At first the villagers were reluctant to talk about it, but slowly they began to realize that remembering and relating the events were bringing them together again. They began coming to Dominique's house to tell what they knew to the men. It seemed that as they remembered and spoke of the horrors and how they felt at the time, it made them feel better, not realizing that it was part of a healing process. Neighbors that hardly spoke to each other since the war ended began talking to each other again. It was almost becoming a festive event, except for Dominique and her family when they realized that the men were going to take the baby back with them.

Each of the villagers' stories were slightly different, but most remembered that night as if it happened yesterday. There were the air raid sirens that sounded off constantly when they had to go into their cellars making sure that all the lights in the house were turned off so the planes would not have a target. They usually ended up spending the whole night there, the younger children often sleeping. The adults rarely got any sleep on those nights. Sometimes the air raid sirens seemed to last for days, and sometimes they would not hear them for weeks at a time.

But that night it was different. It was a cold February night and most of the town was already sleeping. The first sound was of the whistle of the passing train. The townspeople usually did not notice the sound of the trains passing in the night as it was a recurring sound, but on this night as the sound of the approaching train grew nearer, there was another sound increasing in loudness. As the people realized it was the sound of planes, the air raid sirens began to blare. The bombs began to fall as the people hurried to their shelters in the cellars. Then there was that horrendous sound when they knew that the bombs had fallen directly on the train. Not only did they hear the sounds of the bombs, but also the explosions and the crashing of the train as it flew off the tracks and skidded until it finally rested among the vineyards near their homes. After many hours of waiting until the noises of the bombings were over, when it was just a few hours before dawn, the villagers slowly came out of hiding to survey the destruction. They heard the screams and moans and realized that there were survivors. The villagers then began to go through the wreckage to do what they could for those that were still alive. At first, they had to put out the fires before they could get to those that were alive and to the bodies of those that were not.

They soon realized that almost everyone on the train was a German soldier. Those that were badly wounded were taken to the nearby hospital. Those with lesser wounds were treated by the villagers, then sent to a French prison. Even though they were Germans, the villager's compassion for the suffering prevented them from watching the German soldiers slowly die from their wounds.

A baby's cry alerted the rescuers. In the burning wreckage, the villagers discovered a couple of civilian women. They were dead apparently from the fires. Underneath one of the women was a small baby. Because it was covered by the body of one of the women, it was sheltered from the fires. There seemed to be only minor injuries on its arms and legs. If the villagers hadn't found the baby when they did, it certainly would have died as the fires were still burning near it.

Dominique was told to take the child home quickly and tend to its wounds.

The soldiers who were rescued were questioned about the women and baby, but they could not or would not explain who they were. Even amidst the tragedy, the Germans remained stoic.

Since no one knew the identity of the child, the only option was to keep her until they could discover information about the child. They knew, because of the war, it would be a long time away. Dominique's family took over the responsibility of caring for the child even though they did not know if she was German, French, Jewish, or any other nationality. Because of the situation of the war, it did not matter.

Eventually after the war was over, Dominique's family wanted to find out who the baby belonged to, but they had no clue as to where to begin. They asked the Mayor to see what he could do, but as the village was busy rebuilding, he did not have time to make a concerted effort. As they grew fond of her, they raised her as their own child. Dominique treated her as the sister she never had. Three years went by and they came to love the child as their own, believing that no one would ever come to claim her. That would change the day the men came.

Dominique had taken the baby outside to play in the vineyards and was laughing and chasing her around when she heard the car drive up. Two American soldiers got out of the car along with the Mayor. The Mayor was a short jovial man but today he had that serious look she had seen recently. She watched as the two soldiers and the Mayor walked up the path to the house. One of the American soldiers was tall and walked with a cane. She was told that he was severely injured during the war and had to have his leg amputated. His face had scars on the left side from burns. He was the quieter one and always looked sad. The other soldier was shorter, friendlier, but Dominique saw that he also had scars from the war. Even though she hated what they were coming for she did feel sorry for these men. She knew that many American Soldiers came to France and had a big part in freeing their country from the Nazis. Too many had died for a cause that was not their own, including many French civilians. Too many others were wounded as these soldiers were. She knew enough to appreciate what they had done for her country, but she could not forgive them for wanting to take her baby away.

The shorter soldier spoke to her more about the event than the other man did although the taller man listened intently as Dominique told what she remembered. It seemed to Dominique that the men were trying to be friends with her, but she knew that they only wanted to find out as much as she could tell them about the baby. Conversations were difficult at first because the men spoke very little French and Dominique spoke only a little English. The soldier asked a lot about the baby's habits, likes and dislikes. Dominique was the one who was more familiar with the baby's habits because she had become her main caretaker while her parents and brother worked to repair the damage the bombs had done to their vineyard. She had come to love the baby as more than a sister. She was like her own child. Her brother and the rest of her family and neighbors spent most of the last three years out in the fields repairing the damage done by the war from the bombings and the train wreck. They had to replant some of the damaged grape vines, while trying to restore some normalcy back into their lives. Even after three years the village and its people were still recovering. The scars were still visible in the buildings, and on the landscape, and not so visible were the scars deeply rooted in the people's hearts.

"Dominique! Dominique! Viens ici. Maintenant!" She heard her mother call. This was the last day she would be able to spend with the baby. This was the day the soldiers were taking the baby to America. Compared to the days of the war, this was the saddest day of Dominique's life. They had told her not to appear upset so the baby would not cry. She took the baby's hand and slowly walked up to the house. The shorter soldier picked up the baby and asked, "Are her bags packed?"

"Oui, they are upstairs. I go get them now." Dominique answered. She had packed her things

earlier, but was trying to delay the inevitable. She slowly went upstairs to get the baby's things. There wasn't much to the meager belongings, just some clothes and soft toys. Dominique reluctantly packed her new book she liked to read to the baby, "*Le Petit Prince.*" She wanted to send it with the baby hoping that someday the baby would look at the book and remember her. She decided to pack one of the two photographs she had. One was taken by a local reporter of the wreckage and sent to the underground newspaper that the people depended on for the truths of what was happening in all of France. It showed the scene of the wreckage but did not include pictures of her family. The other photo was the one her neighbor took that was a picture of the family a year later. It was of her holding the baby, along with her parents, and her two brothers. Just after that picture was taken, her older brother was sent to Germany as part of a work program. They were told that he would return after the war and they were still waiting for him. It was the only picture she had of him and was reluctant to part with it, but sentiments aside, she wanted the baby to have it. She decided to put the family photograph inside the back lining of the book hoping it would not be thrown away and that someday the baby would find the picture and ask about the family in the photograph. She kept the photograph of the newspaper account of the train wreck.

When she went back downstairs, the men were ready to leave. Her family had all said their goodbys, but when it came to her turn, she started crying and hugging the baby. She just couldn't believe that she would never see her again. She didn't want to let go. "*Don't take her please!*" she wailed. But it was to no avail. Dominique went to the upstairs window and watched until she could no longer see the car that drove her baby away. She put her face to the window and said quietly, "*Au revoir ma petite.*"

PART ONE

CHAPTER ONE

Sophie St. Pierre was finishing her lunch on the bench in Audubon Park across from Tulane University where she was a student. It was a quiet place where she often studied in between classes. Sometimes she enjoyed just sitting under the old oak and magnolia trees watching the ducks in the lagoons and birds and children flitting around busily going about their daily activities. She savored the peaceful feeling that this solitude generated in her. She didn't like the noisy student center even though most of her friends studied there. She couldn't get used to the constant interruptions of people coming from and going to class. It was a great place to socialize, but Sophie was a more serious student and wanted to get the best grades she could in her journalism classes. On days like this when the weather was almost perfect, just cool enough for a sweater, she would take her lunch to the park and feed the leftovers to the ducks. When she was studying, she was usually oblivious to her surroundings.

On this beautiful November afternoon, she finished her lunch and was on her way back to her last class of the day. As she walked back to campus, she stopped at the streetcar tracks in the neutral ground to let the car pass by. She hardly noticed the metallic sound of the streetcar as it stopped to let off students and take on more. The odor of the old brass fixtures in the streetcar wafted by, but her awareness was on other things. Her final exams were coming up soon and she was going over the information she had studied while in the park. The afternoon was unusually quiet, but she didn't notice. She was always deeply in thought with her eyes to the ground most of the time, often running into things or people. She got to her building and walked up the old steps where ivy was invading in between the cracks and climbing up the walls finding tiny strongholds to cling to. She didn't notice the musty smell inside the old building since she was used to it. She got to her classroom and found a seat in the center of the room, opening her book, still not aware that no one else was there. There was a buzzing of chatter in the halls but she didn't pay attention to it. Suddenly she became aware that the noise in the hall was more than the usual sound of students scurrying to get to their classes. It was a louder commotion and a mixture of sobs and cries. As Sophie was becoming aware that something unpleasant was happening, a few students entered the classroom along with the professor. They had a horrible troubled look on their faces and some were crying. Then the world stood still as he announced,

"President Kennedy is dead! He was assassinated in Dallas. I have no other information than that. Classes are canceled until further notice."

Sophie didn't remember how she got to the student union after that, all she remembered was that she was standing with her friends and everyone was staring at the television. Disbelief was on their faces, as some were sobbing, others just staring as if in some trance waiting to be awakened. No one knew what to say. Sophie felt at that moment the world had changed. The world that she knew was a sheltered one where nothing bad happened. Horrible events were things you only read about in history books. Wars, assassinations, natural disasters, all of those things happened somewhere else, in some other time, never here and now in this her quiet and perfect world where everyone was happy and dreams always came true.

She grew up in a quiet uptown area in a house on Octavia Street near Audubon Park. She was an only child and was given everything she wanted and needed, went to good schools, and had a few close friends that she had known since kindergarten. She was not the most popular girl but never wanted to be. She was not spoiled, but never lacked for anything. Her life was stable and secure, set on a path that she thought would always be comfortable. She didn't argue with her parents and accepted that she would go to Tulane University after high school. She liked writing and taking photographs, so it was natural for her to major in Journalism. She expected that she would get married, have children and live a normal prosperous life. She hoped to work in Journalism, but not as a full time career. She and her best friend Theresa often discussed what their futures would be as married women with a few children, good husband, and a good home life. They would marry their boyfriends after graduating from collage and life would be great. And normal.

Something changed on that November day when President John F. Kennedy was shot. Her comfortable world was shattered. There was no social unrest in the country, nor was there a war. The country seemed to be going in a positive direction and most of the people she knew were happy. She had never known death in her family, had never been to a funeral. She never knew her grandparents and so never experienced their death. She was told little about them, only that one of them had died in World War II. Other people died like famous movie stars, mostly old people, but no one that she particularly admired or was close to. And she knew of no accidents that had killed young people. But this was different. This was something that didn't make sense, that a young well loved energetic person, vibrant and alive, with a beautiful family, the President of the United States, with hopes and dreams for a future in America that was going to be extraordinary. How could he, surrounded by police and secret service men, be shot and killed by an unknown insignificant individual right in the middle of a motorcade in a safe American city. This would be the first small tear in the comfort and normalcy of her subconscious that would change the way she thought of her life and security.

For days the students and the nation watched their televisions for every bit of information on the assassination and the funeral. They watched in horror as Lee Harvey Oswald was shot and murdered by Jack Ruby live on TV. They watched the funeral as the Kennedy family marched down the avenue. Then at the grave site, they watched as little John Jr. saluted his father. There was not a dry eye in the nation on that day.

Gradually life returned to normal as classes resumed and the nation settled with a new president, but there was a more serious and solemn attitude in the background of everyone's lives. While the holidays were celebrated as usual, and the memories of the assassination seemed to fade, there was a darkness lurking behind everyone's consciousness. There was an internal expectation of what the next horrific event was going to be.

Sophie had finished school that December. She had started college the summer after high school, and continued taking courses each summer, with the intention to graduate early, without understanding why, thinking that she just liked going to school and studying. The graduation ceremony would be in May, since not many students finished school in the middle of the year. It was a cold January day just before the next semester began when Sophie's friend Theresa came over with exciting news. "He proposed!" Tessa showed Sophie her ring. "Geoffrey and I are going to get married right after graduation." she said. "I will have my degree in teaching so I'm going to work while Geoff goes to medical school."

"That's wonderful news," said Sophie. "I guess Wayne will get me a ring soon. But I don't know about getting married right away. I think we should wait a while until we get jobs."

"Why wait? We've decided there's no reason to wait. We might as well start our lives together. Waiting is just that, waiting. Imagine that! We will be Dr. and Mrs. Geoffrey Wolff. This is so exciting, planning for a wedding and everything." Tessa said. "You will be my Maid of Honor, won't you Sophie?"

"Of course. Come spend the weekend with me and we can look at ideas for dresses." said Sophie. "My parents are going out of town so it will be quiet."

"Where are they going?" asked Tessa.

"We usually go to Chicago or New York every year, but this time I am not going with them. I just want to relax and enjoy the fact that I don't have to study anymore. Besides I sent out a resume to the *Times Picayune* for a job as a reporter and actually have an interview next week."

"Well your Journalism degree should be impressive. Your grades and all the articles you wrote for our school paper ought to count for something. I remember the one you wrote after President Kennedy was assassinated. Everyone thought that was the best piece you had ever written."

"Thanks. Let me know tomorrow if you can come over this weekend. My parents will feel more comfortable knowing that I won't be alone. This will be the first time I don't go with them."

"What do you do in Chicago and New York?" asked Tessa.

"My mother takes me to museums and other places while my father attends to business. I don't know what he does there, but it seems to be important. We usually go to one place or the other each year."

"That sounds exciting. My family only goes to visit my aunt in Virginia every summer. We drive through the mountains, but that's about it."

"That would be a great place to take pictures, all those mountains." said Sophie.

"We don't take many pictures, just a couple with family. It is pretty though, you would take great photographs. You are good at that. I don't even own a camera."

"My father gave me my camera when I was ten. I try to take a different kind of picture than the usual. I have a few from our vacations. I like to experiment by taking pictures of things people don't usually take pictures of, like scenery and buildings, kind of like Ansel Adams does."

"You already do that. Your photographs in our paper are more creative than any others I've seen."

"Thanks for the compliment. But I'd like to get better. So you will spend the weekend with me?"

Sophie and Tessa had grown up together. Sophie never felt like an only child because she and Tessa spent so much time together along with Tessa's brother and little sister. They were best friends in elementary school and high school. Although they were very different in their appearance, they were similar in the way they studied and took life seriously. Sophie was tall and slim with a light complexion that burned if she spent only a few minutes in the sun. Her blond hair was long and wavy and she wore pastel clothes that accented her blue-green eyes. Tessa was short and not quite overweight, but had a tendency to be if she didn't watch her diet. Her hair was dark and straight and her light brown eyes seemed to glow almost as if they were golden. She usually wore earthy colors as she was not daring enough to be show-offy with bright colors or too much make-up. They shared almost everything with each other and enjoyed spending the night at each other's homes. They even called each other's mother their "other mother". They felt perfectly at ease with each others' family.

Sophie and Tessa spent Friday night discussing wedding plans. On Saturday after they ate breakfast and looked through many bridal magazines they were ready for a break. Tessa said,

"Hey I'm tired of looking at wedding dresses, they're beginning to all look alike. Lets take a break and do something different."

"Like what?" asked Sophie.

"Remember when we used to go rooting around in your attic and play dress-up in your mother's old clothes and all the Mardi Gras costumes?"

"That was fun." agreed Sophie. "What? You want to play dress-up? Aren't we a little old for that?"

"No, I just like going into your attic. There's interesting stuff there. Lets go explore."

"Ok, I haven't been up there in a while. I might find something interesting to put back in my room."

The attic was the top floor of an old raised house in an old neighborhood near Audubon Park. There were many mansions in her neighborhood, but Sophie's house was one of the smaller houses. It was one story not counting the attic. All of the houses had attics as there was no way to build a basement under the swampy ground that the city was built on. The small porch had four columns topped with gingerbread designs, and a swing attached to the ceiling. There wasn't much of a yard but there was a tiny shed in the back for her father's tools. There was no garage so cars were parked on the street. Sophie's parents owned only one car. Since they were a few blocks from St. Charles Avenue, they rode the streetcars everywhere. The wrought iron fence off the sidewalk was decorated with fleur-de-lis on top of each post. French doors with shutters opened into the large living/dining room. A chandelier hung from the high ceiling over the dining room table. The house was built in the late 1800's using cypress wood. The house was still in its original shape except for the kitchen which was remodeled. Sophie's bedroom was large and she had an armoire for her clothes. There were no closets built in the old homes. She had a four poster bed, with a dresser and vanity table to match. Her walls were decorated with flowery wallpaper. There was only one bathroom that had tiny black and white tiles on the floor, and an old clawfoot bathtub.

The attic had an old musty smell of stale odors. There was a pull down stairs in the ceiling of the hallway. It gave a creaking sound as they pulled down the stairs. There were two single hanging lightbulbs on each end of the attic that gave little light to the dim room. There was enough room to stand in the center, and on each side were boxes of clothes, old furniture, and a metal file cabinet that was usually locked.

Sophie was looking through a box of old school stuff and wasn't watching what Tessa was doing. Tessa was looking through the file cabinet. It wasn't locked. It contained a lot of personal information. "Look at this." said Tessa. "It looks like your parent's marriage certificate."

"Hey, that's their personal stuff. Put that back."

"Ok, sorry, but wait. Look back here at this file. It has your name on it."

"It's probably just my birth certificate, and health information." said Sophie. As they glanced through the files Sophie was looking at the records. "I've seen all this before. Just put it back."

Tessa was sliding the file back into place when she noticed a file towards the back with a name on it she didn't recognize. "Look at this file, Sophie. It's a file for someone named 'Phillip'. Do you know anyone named Phillip?"

"No, I never heard of a Phillip."

"Could it be one of your grandfathers or your uncle or cousin?"

"I don't have any cousins. My parents are both only children, just like me. Maybe it's a grandfather. I never knew my grandparents. In fact, I don't even remember if they told me their first names. I was told that they had all died before I was born. My parents were both older when I was born."

"Then let's look in it."

"I guess it will be ok. Let's take it out."

Tessa opened the folder. As they both were scanning through the papers, Tessa found a birth certificate. "Hey, here is a birth certificate for this Phillip. Let's see who he is."

Sophie saw it first. When Tessa noticed it, they both were shocked. "This is the same birthday as yours!" exclaimed Tessa. "Same year, same day, December 24, Christmas Eve, and your parents are listed as his parents. It's like he's your twin or something."

Sophie paled as she read the date on the certificate. She saw that the names of the parents were her own. "I don't understand. I'm not a twin. They never told me I had a twin."

"But it is your parents names and your birth date. It has to be your twin brother. Maybe he died at birth. See if there is a death certificate in here."

Sophie felt uneasy about looking through her parents personal papers, but curiosity kept her from putting them back. She wanted to know who this was. Then they found the boy's death certificate. He died shortly after he was born. "He didn't live one day." she said. "But this doesn't make sense. They don't have 'twin' on the certificate. Not on his or on mine. I thought they had to write on the certificate if it was twins."

"Your parents never told you about this?" asked Tessa.

"No. They never said anything." Sophie felt confused, a little angry, and a sense of loss at a twin brother she never knew she had. "Tessa, you can't tell anyone about this. Please tell me you won't tell anyone. Please. I don't know what I am going to do, but you can't tell. I have to think about this and what I should do about it."

"I won't tell, I promise. But are you going to ask you parents about this?"

"I don't know. I don't know why they felt like I shouldn't know about this. Maybe they thought I wasn't ready, or couldn't handle it, or maybe it never seemed like the right time. I just have to think about this first. I just need time to think. Put the papers back. Make sure it doesn't look like we went through them. Let's go downstairs. I don't want to be up here anymore."

"There are more papers behind these. I see some sort of book back there. Don't you want to look through these to see if you can find out more?"

"No. Put them back. I just had this shocking information and I have to think about it. I don't want any more surprises right now. Maybe I'll look in there later, but not now."

"I'm really sorry Sophie. I was just having fun looking through old stuff."

Sophie didn't sleep well that night. The next day she pretended to be interested in Tessa's wedding plans, but kept staring at the same page thinking about the birth certificate they found for Phillip, and if she should confront her parents about it. She didn't feel comfortable telling her parents that she was snooping around in their private papers. But she felt she needed an answer to who Phillip was and why they didn't tell her.

She had forgotten that their boyfriends were coming by that afternoon and she nearly jumped out of her skin when she heard the doorbell ring. "Hey you two, time to take a break." said Geoff.

"Let's go out for dinner, then go to the movies. Do y'all want to go see *It's a Mad, Mad, Mad, Mad World*? I've been wanting to see that movie since it came out." said Wayne, Sophie's boyfriend.

Sophie had known Wayne since they were children going to the same schools. They began dating in high school. To everyone they were the ideal couple. It was inevitable that they would someday get married. It seemed to their friends that they belonged together. Sophie and Wayne were more serious about their studies and their future, although they did go out with their friends drinking and partying.

"That's a great idea." said Tessa.

"Yes. I've been wanting to see that too. We've been studying so hard, I think we need to get out and have some fun." said Geoff.

"No, I don't feel up to it. Why don't y'all go?" said Sophie.

Tessa nudged Sophie as she said under her breath so their boyfriends wouldn't hear, "We both really need to get out. Come on Sophie, I know you can't stop thinking about who Phillip is, but you should get your mind off of that and get out for some fun. Besides you can't do anything about it until your parents get back"

Sophie realized that Tessa was right, so she agreed. At first during the movie, Sophie couldn't stop thinking of who Phillip was, but soon began to pay attention to the movie and was even laughing with the rest of the audience. After that they went to Café Du Monde and had café au lait and beignets. Sophie was laughing again as she almost forgot about Phillip. It was late when they rode the streetcar back to Sophie's house. Tessa and Geoff went to the kitchen for hot chocolate. Wayne and Sophie were sitting on the sofa. He began kissing her, and just when Sophie was about to stop him from going further, he stopped and surprised her, "Sophie, I love you. I want to get married. Will you marry me?"

Although she was expecting him to ask her, she was still startled. "Yes, yes." was all that she could say.

"We can plan our wedding for this May after we all graduate. Maybe we can get married before Tessa and Geoff," Wayne said.

"That's really too soon." Sophie said. "I have an interview next week and don't know if I will have a job at the newspaper or not. And you don't have a job yet either. Don't you have an interview with a bank?"

"It's with Magnolia Bank and they will probably hire me."

"Then let's wait until both of our interviews are over." Sophie wasn't ready to commit to getting married yet. She wasn't sure she really wanted to be married to Wayne. She thought that that was what was expected of her, to get married after graduation like ever other woman and start a family. She thought that she loved him, but to spend the rest of their lives together, have kids and a house and be settled, she just didn't know if she could do that yet. She felt that there was something she needed to do first, but what that was she didn't know. And because of her discovery in the attic, she felt there was something more she needed to know or do before planning her future.

Sophie arrived at the interview early. She looked around at the workings of the newspaper, a little surprised at how noisy it was. She was led down a long narrow hallway to the personnel office, a smaller room filled with stacks of papers in every corner.

"Your resume is impressive." Mrs. Myers commented. "We already have a few people who do free lancework for us. It doesn't pay much because we pay by the article. Right now we have all the bases covered in each department. There might be an opening across the lake in Mandeville soon, if you would like to take that position. Why don't you check back with me in a month or so."

Sophie was disappointed, but felt that she shouldn't have expected a job right away. This wasn't a job like Tessa was getting where there were a lot of openings for teachers. As she was thanking Mrs. Myers, there was a knock on the door. Before Mrs. Myers could get up to answer it, the door flung open and a loud hefty woman barged in. "Patty, I see you're hardly working as usual." The lady's loud voice startled Sophie.

"Same as you. Same as you, you old dog." answered Patty Myers, obviously pleased to see her friend. "What brings you here?"

"We just wrapped up an article about the Atchafalaya Basin and the Cajun groups of people who make their living in the area. Thought we'd come by to say hi. Whose the pretty young lady you've got here? Reporters are getting younger and prettier every day. I should think of retiring soon."

"That'll be the day. You can't quit, you love the job too much. This pretty young lady is Sophie St. Pierre. She wants to be a reporter here. Sophie, meet Doris. She, Jack, and Leonard do most of the free lance work for *The WorldView* magazine. They travel all over the world writing extensive articles for the magazine."

Sophie stood up to shake hands with Doris, "I know the magazine. It's excellent. I've read most of the articles you wrote. It's an honor to meet you."

"So how's your crew?" asked Mrs. Myers.

"We're all good. Jack is leaving though. He got tired of traveling and missed being away from his family for our long assignments, so he took a position to help run one of California's newest attempts at a newspaper."

"Good for him. He'll do well. Give him my best. How long will you be in town?"

"We'll stay a few days to wrap up our story and add the finishing touches on it. Our next assignment is in Alaska. We are going to some small villages where there is still a small Eskimo population. We want to document some of their customs before they become completely civilized and their way of life is lost forever."

Sophie wanted to get a word in before she left, "The way you incorporate history and geography with the people and current events of the areas you write about is impressive. Thank you Mrs. Myers for the interview. I should be going now."

"You must read *The WorldView* a lot to understand how we write our articles," replied Doris obviously impressed.

"Yes I do. I learned a lot about writing and photography by reading them." said Sophie.

"So you are applying for a job as a reporter? Patty, can I see her resume?" Doris looked through the paperwork and at Sophie's photographs. "Not bad for a beginner. You could use some hands on training. You know we are going to be a man short until we can replace Jack. Would you be interested in coming with us to Alaska?"

Sophie was startled. "Are you serious? That would be fantastic. I would love to go!" She surprised herself by her immediate and enthusiastic response.

"What do you think Patty? Can I steal your next great reporter from you?" Doris teased.

"We don't have an opening here right now anyway. It would be good training for her if she wants to go."

Doris and Sophie exchanged phone numbers. "Go think about it and talk to your family. I'll call you in a few days with the plans and see if you really want to do this."

As Sophie rode home in the streetcar looking out the window at the Mansions along St. Charles Avenue, Sophie's thoughts were racing. She began thinking seriously about getting married and about the offer to go to Alaska. *What am I doing? I was going to get married, have a family, live a nice normal life. Is that really what I want? I can go to Alaska. I've never been anywhere on my own before. But I wouldn't exactly be on my own. Doris is an excellent writer and I could learn a lot from her. Going to Alaska is scary. But getting married and starting a future with Wayne is scary too. I haven't really thought much about my future before except that I'll get married and have a normal family life because that's what I am expected to do. And what about my interest in becoming a journalist? Is that just going to be like a hobby because I'll be busy with a family? Or do I want to do more with my life than get married, have a family, and a nice little hobby to keep busy. That can't be all there is. Yes I want to go to Alaska. It's a one time thing. It will be exciting. I'll take lots of pictures and always have that to remember before I settle down.*

Wayne was upset. They had just come from one of the Mardi Gras parades with their friends and were sitting in Wayne's parent's kitchen having hot cocoa. He lived near the parade route down the street from St. Charles Avenue. Most of their friends lived in the neighborhood and had gone to the same schools together since they were children. They usually caught the parades and ended up at one of their houses afterward while their parents fixed hot chocolate for them. When they were nearly finished drinking their cocoa and the conversations lagged Sophie decided that was the time to announce her plans to go to Alaska. Everyone looked at Sophie with surprise and had positive comments about the trip. Except for Wayne. "You want to go to Alaska with a couple of strangers? What about us? What about our plans? What's wrong with you, are you crazy?"

"Why are you so upset? These strangers are the experts in photojournalism. I'll be learning things

I never could in a classroom. I will be gaining experience. This is the opportunity of a lifetime. I can't pass this up. Anyway it's only for a couple of weeks.

"You don't know these people! You don't know what can happen. Some strangers invite you to go to Alaska and you say ok? What's wrong with you?"

"They are not strangers. I met them at the *Times Picayune*. They are professionals and people at the newspaper know them, and I happen to know who they are because I read their names in the articles in *The WorldView*. So they are not strangers, they are people who are at the top of the field in photojournalism. I'm honored that they asked me to go with them. This is an experience that I can not pass up. Why can't you understand that?"

"You can't go. I won't let you!"

"You won't let me? We aren't married yet. You can't tell me what I can or can't do."

"You're right about that!" Wayne replied getting angrier. "Go ahead, go on that stupid trip of yours. But don't expect me to be happy about it."

All of their friends looked at each other and conveniently made excuses to leave. There were hardly ever any arguments between any of them so this was an unexpected development, and they all didn't quite know how to react except to let them talk about it with each other. After their friends left, Sophie resumed the conversation. "It's not a stupid trip. It's important to me to do this and I'll only be gone for a couple of weeks. I'll write you and call when I can. I'll be back before you know it. Then we can plan our wedding."

As soon as she said it, Sophie had a strange feeling of dread. *Married? I'll be a married woman?*

And have children? I'm not sure I'm ready for that. Maybe this is the best thing that could have happened. I'm going to go out into the real world, see a part of life that I only read about and see places I've only seen in magazines. I'm excited and scared, but I feel that this is the what I need to do. I'll think about Wayne and getting married after I get back. And there's the problem of asking my parents about who Philip is. I've been afraid to confront them about it because I don't know how to ask them without telling them that Tessa and I went through their private papers. Maybe I can get some advise from someone else. Maybe I can talk to Doris about it.

CHAPTER TWO

Sophie looked out of the window of the plane as it approached the runway. "So beautiful. All that snow. I never imagined it was so beautiful. We don't get much snow in New Orleans."

"Yes, I know." said Doris. "What you see out there is only the beginning."

The entire plane ride Sophie couldn't stop looking out the window of the plane. She was amazed that she was really going to Alaska. As she watched the patterns of the landscape below change as they flew over cities, plains, valleys, mountains, then the snow covered mountains through Canada, Sophie's thoughts went back to the events that brought her here. She came home one afternoon a few days after her interview and found Doris and Leonard at her house talking with her parents. They had already made the travel arrangements and left Sophie with instructions, what to pack and when to meet them at the airport. What she feared the most was that her parents would say that she couldn't go. But they agreed easily, almost too easily, Sophie thought. She had discussed with them about marrying Wayne and if they would be disappointed if she didn't marry him soon and start a family. But they told her that it was her decision and she needed to do what she felt was best for her. It was her future and she was the only one who could decide about what felt right for her. There would be plenty of time since she is so young, they said, that making a commitment to get married would be a lifetime commitment and harder to change if she wanted to choose a different path.

Her parents seemed different after they returned from their trip to New York, when Sophie had discovered the birth certificate for Phillip. They couldn't have known what she had found. Sophie thought maybe their attitude was different because she was out of collage now and needed to decide on her own future as an adult. Maybe her parents saw her as grown woman now and Sophie was now in charge of her own life, not that she felt like a grown woman. Because she was planning this trip to Alaska, Sophie decided not to mention what she found in the attic. She wasn't sure how to bring it up anyway without telling them that she was snooping into their personal things.

She had more trouble convincing Wayne to let her go. Sophie was upset that Wayne felt that he had to give her permission to go. They weren't married yet but he was acting like important decisions were to be made by him without any input from her. As the time came closer to the date of departure, she and Wayne became more distant. They didn't have as much fun as before. Sophie decided that Wayne was just upset that she was leaving, and maybe a little jealous. She dismissed their disagreement as just that, a little spat. Her friend Tessa thought it was a fantastic opportunity. Tessa and Geoff were already starting to plan their lives, looking for an apartment to move into right after the wedding. Tessa was accepted for a job teaching first grade in a Catholic School. They were going to live on her salary while Geoff went to medical school. Sophie thought they seemed happy and settled, but Sophie didn't feel ready for that kind of commitment yet. She was glad that this opportunity came up or else she would probably be planning a wedding that she wasn't sure she was ready for.

As the scenery changed below the clouds, Sophie became more excited about this adventure. She was looking down at the most astounding view, nothing like she had ever seen on the trips to New York and Chicago. Endless mountains of incredible height covered with snow. Dark green pines shooting up from the valleys between the mountains. Whites with blue shadows as far as she could see. Only a hint of cities or civilization could be seen now and then in between miles and miles of snow, beautiful and lonely. She got her camera out and started taking pictures from the window of the plane.

"Don't use up all your film in the plane." Doris laughed.

"This is the most amazing scenery I have ever seen." Sophie said.

"This is only the beginning." Doris said. "There is so much more to come, so go ahead and take all the photos you want. You can always buy more film in Anchorage."

"You must live the most exciting life, going all over the world, constantly seeing new places, meeting new people." said Sophie.

"It is exciting, but sometimes it gets to be routine. And sometimes we're so busy that we don't always get to enjoy the places we visit."

"How did you get to work for *The WorldView*?" Sophie asked.

Doris explained how she started in the business. She wrote stories in a local paper for years before she was offered a job as an assistant with a national magazine. Soon she became a lead writer. Then at a convention she had met Leonard. He was becoming acclaimed as a photographer, just as she was moving up in the world of acclaimed writers. They were impressed with each others' works and hoped to be able to work together someday. Then seven years ago, they were both offered a job independently at *The WorldView,* met again at the magazine's main office, and decided to work together. They needed a third person to work with them but couldn't keep anyone for more than a couple of years as it was a tough job with so much traveling and being away from family for so long. Jack worked with them for the last two and a half years, but he always wanted to go back to his home in California.

Len was sitting across from them in the plane. He did not join in the conversation. He hadn't talked to Sophie much at all. Sophie got the impression that Len did not want her with them, or that he didn't like her, but she didn't feel comfortable discussing that with Doris.

"We've landed now Sophie, you can wake up from your reverie." Doris was getting her luggage down from the overhead bin.

"Oh, I'm sorry, I couldn't take my eyes off the scenery outside. I can't believe I'm really here."

"It is beautiful. After we get settled in the hotel, we can do some sightseeing. We have a day to spend before we go visiting outlying areas."

After checking into the hotel, Doris, Len and Sophie met the mayor of Anchorage for a tour. Sophie could barely hold her excitement about everything especially the scenery. The snow everywhere was so deep she kept picking up handfuls of it even tasting it. The mountains in the distance were so majestic that Sophie felt euphoric. The air was so crisp and cold and dry she could feel it's sharpness in her lungs, unlike the humid air of the South. She took so many pictures she already had to buy more film. After they ate and returned to the hotel, Doris told Sophie to get a good night's sleep as they would have an early start in the morning. Sophie was so excited she hardly slept, spending most of the night looking out at the colors that the city lights made in the night snow. Feelings that she had never felt before along with the excitement of this new adventure, Sophie felt as if she were being awakened to a new awareness of life.

The villagers of the little town of Afognak welcomed the visitors with excitement and curiosity. It looked like the whole town was lined up near the dock as they got out of the seaplane. The children circled around them laughing and touching their clothes. Sophie had her camera ready and started snapping pictures of them. The villagers led them to a small building that resembled a hut but was actually their post office. Doris and Len interviewed as many people as would talk to them. Sophie watched the way Doris made it seem as if she were having a pleasant conversation with the villagers, not taking notes, but had a small tape recorder inside her coat. Len was taking pictures as he wandered around. At first many of the villagers stared at Len and some posed for the pictures, but after they were there a few days, the people went about their business and Len took casual photos of them. The children followed Len around as some of them had never seen a camera before. But they soon got bored and went about their daily activities.

Much of the villagers' lives were involved with fishing. They mostly caught salmon but sometimes larger prey when in season. Sophie watched as they went out in their kayaks and brought back fish. Although the villagers didn't have much in the way of modern conveniences, they seemed content with their lives. They didn't need television because they entertained themselves; they didn't need toys, knickknacks or all the stuff that fills the houses of other Americans because they made everything they had and everything they had was useful. All of the so-called modern conveniences that were supposed to make life easier but only took more time to use and keep working well, were completely useless to these villagers. They loved and enjoyed life as no one she had ever met did. Everyone helped everyone else, they all had their job to do, even the children, and they each did it well. Sophie felt a peacefulness similar to the feelings she had in her solitude at Audubon Park. Watching the villagers at their daily routine, and taking in the scenery around her, the mountains, the waters, the snow, Sophie thought what a wonderful way to live, so different from what she had known, yet with such purpose and contentment, these people were happy.

They then traveled to another small town called Portage, which was a small railroad town of less than a hundred rugged men. These were the men who helped build the railroads. There were no women or children as life was too hard to bring wives and children here, but the men often went back to the city where their families sometimes stayed. The men weren't very talkative and explained what they did in very few words. Doris got some of them to talk about where they came from and why they wanted to work in such a desolate place. Mostly it was for the money. They were making a lot of it and some of them intended to work a few years, save a lot of money and return home to start a better life. Some of them were rugged construction workers from their home town and were used to hard work. Those that weren't, didn't last long.

After spending a couple of weeks visiting many different towns and villages, they returned to Anchorage. Sophie was amazed at the differences of the people in each town. The Natives who were trying to hold on to their ancestral ways, the rugged men who were there to build the future, and the modern Americans in the city who came from the lower 48 for a new way of life. There were so many differences in cultures all within a few hundred miles of each other, that Sophie was overwhelmed. She felt that her life had been so sheltered that it bordered on boring. She thought that a life like Doris and Len had traveling around the world seeing how others lived and visiting strange and exotic places was the most wonderful life anyone could have.

At the hotel, after they finished packing for the return trip home the next day, they went out to meet the Mayor who was treating them to a farewell dinner. As they were walking toward the restaurant they felt a rumble through the ground. They stopped and looked at each other nervously. All the locals on the street stopped as they waited for the tremor to stop as they were used to this happening, and people nearby said to them "That's just a tremor from an earthquake. We get that all the time, nothing to worry about. Just wait a few minutes and it will stop."

But the tremor didn't stop. Instead the ground started violently shaking and the noise increased. People started yelling then screams of terror rang out. The Mayor ran to them from the restaurant and pulled them into the street as some of the buildings started to collapse. "Stay here until it's over, it's safer here in the street," he said as he ran off to see who else he could help.

They were unable to stand and ended up half sitting, half lying down as the shaking grew worse and bricks and other debris tumbled down. Sophie couldn't believe what she was seeing and feeling. On one side of them the ruined buildings seemed to be falling into the earth while on the other side they seemed to be rising. "What's happening?" She screamed along with Doris and Len. The terror went on and on and when they thought the end of the world was at hand, it stopped. They didn't know if more was coming so they didn't dare move. As they looked around people were beginning to stand, then run to where the street fell in to see if they could be of help.

Unbelievable sights were all around them. The sidewalk where they were just walking seemed to have disappeared. It had fallen along with all the buildings on that side six or seven feet into the ground. There were huge cracks in the street where cars and people had fallen into. With a reporters instinct, Len grabbed his camera and started taking pictures, first from his position on the ground, then daring to stand up. Doris turned on her tape recorder and started dictating into it. Sophie had her camera with her and tentatively at first started taking pictures too. Then she stood up with Doris and Len. She aimed the camera everywhere and anywhere, at the devastation, at the people running, and at the terrorized faces of the adults and children nearby.

When they had eventually run out of film and tapes, they carefully returned to their hotel. It seemed to be intact, but the manager wouldn't let them back in. He explained that there would be many aftershocks and it was too dangerous. Doris convinced him to let them return to their room because they had expensive equipment to check on and they would be quick. He reluctantly agreed but warned them that they were on their own and he would not take responsibility for them or any other damage that would occur. He told them that all the other guests were told to evacuate the building until the damages could be accessed and that they needed to return outside as quickly as possible. They were told what shelter to report to when they were done.

Many people were being taken to Elmendorf Air Force Base nearby, since the Anchorage airport was damaged. The fact that the military personnel there were well trained for many unusual situations including disasters, they were well prepared to help out. After Doris, Len and Sophie grabbed their camera equipment and as much of their stuff as they could carry, they were driven to the base. Doris and Len were not concerned about not being able to return home, but they knew that Sophie's parents were planning on meeting them at the airport, so Doris asked about the phone lines. Most of the lines were out, but they eventually found a connection at the army base where they were told to go. After

Sophie spoke to her parents and told them to contact Wayne, Doris informed them that they did not know when they would be allowed to leave since the Anchorage airport was damaged could not be used, and most of the transportation at the Elmendorf base was involved in getting the injured out and supplies in. Sophie wanted to stay as long as Doris and Len were staying, and she really didn't have a choice since only the wounded were being flown out. While she was terrified, she was also intoxicated with excitement and wanted to be in the action.

When she thought there couldn't be any more action, it was announced that tsunamis were hitting along the coast and more devastation was occurring. They were told that the village they visited before was wiped out by a tsunami and most probably all the people were dead. Sophie felt a chill up her spine. All the people they spoke to, all the people they took pictures of, all the children, all of them gone. Their lives that Sophie thought were so perfect, and then out of nowhere, they were wiped out. Everything that they were, did, thought and worked for was taken out with one mighty sweep erased from the face of the earth, gone. It reminded her of when President Kennedy was assassinated, but different in that his being shot was a deliberate act by another human, but this event was caused by Nature Herself. The why of it made no more sense to her. It felt to Sophie that people and nature could not bear a peaceful and calm co-existence, and that when life became serene and complacent, things had to be shaken up. Sophie sat down and cried, "We were just there." she cried. "All those people, and the children, they're gone, just like that. They were so alive, living their lives and, and, now gone? I don't understand it. Why?" Sophie knew things like that happened all over the world, but not to people she met and knew, people she became friends with, the whole village, everything they had, everything they were just wiped out, gone forever.

"There are no answers Sophie. It just happens. You just accept it and go on." Doris, who seemed impervious to emotions, cried too and hugged Sophie, comforting her. Len turned and walked away.

They spent the next few days on the base but returned to the city to help in any way they could. While Doris and Len were doing interviews and taking photos, Sophie spent most of her time helping with the children who were gathered in large rooms at the base, while their parents helped in the city. People who had survived the earthquake and tsunami were arriving. Small planes were flying over the devastation but since they couldn't land, they would drop supplies to anyone they saw needed help. Doris had arranged for the three of them to fly with one of the pilots so they could take more photographs. They tried not to get in the way of the help, but many in charge were aware that documentation of the event was important so they had no trouble getting permission to go along with the rescue crews.

After spending the next week there documenting as much as they could and helping as much as was needed, they decided that it was time to return home. Some of the planes that were bringing supplies were empty on returning to other places since most of the injured were already lifted out, so Doris was able to secure passage to Seattle. There they got tickets to return to New Orleans. On the plane, Doris complemented Sophie on how she handled herself by not complaining about conditions they encountered in the remote towns or by panicking during the earthquake. Sophie told her that that was the most exciting, wonderful, and terrible experience that she had ever had.

The plane ride home would be long and since Sophie had spent the last few weeks with Doris, she felt more comfortable talking to her and decided that she would discuss the information that she and Tessa had found in her attic. She told Doris the whole story about what they had discovered in the attic. Sophie said that she was unsure how or if she should approach her parents about it. "What do you think I should do?" she asked Doris.

Doris remained quiet during Sophie's explanation and to answer her question, she wasn't sure what to advise her to do, so she merely replied, "I'm not sure. I think you should think about why they kept this a secret. Maybe they were going to tell you, but the time never seemed right. Maybe the papers that you saw were not what you think they were about. After all you and your friend Tessa were in a dark attic and you were upset about Tessa going through your parents' private papers. I don't think you should go back and reread the papers, and I don't think you should talk to your parents about this just yet. Give it more time. Maybe they will tell you about it one day. But for now, I wouldn't say anything."

"I guess you're right. It's not something I have to find out about right away. I'll leave it alone for now. Maybe they will tell me about it on their own terms. Thanks Doris. Thanks for everything. Thanks for the opportunity to take this trip with you. I'll never forget it."

Telling her friends about her adventure was almost as exciting as the adventure, and all of them were amazed except Wayne. They had just enjoyed a beautiful spring day at Ponchartrain Beach and were having a picnic by the lake. Later when they were alone, Wayne told her that he hoped she "Got it out of her system."

"What do you mean, 'Got it out of my system?'" Sophie asked.

"Now that your little adventure is over, can we now get to planning our wedding?" Wayne commented as more of a statement then a question.

"My little adventure? I'm not sure I want to plan a wedding right now if you don't understand what this 'adventure' meant to me. We are all graduating next month, and there is Tessa and Geoff's wedding. There is too much going on just now. Let's just wait till all that is over with and we will talk about it again." Sophie said a little testily.

Later that day, when Sophie returned home, her mother told her that Doris called and wanted Sophie to meet her at the *Times Picayune* office in the morning.

"Sophie, glad you could come. I wanted you to see how all our photographs came out. And I was hoping you could look over the story Len and I wrote to see if you think we covered everything. Actually the editor decided that he wanted to devote the entire next issue to our Alaska stories and the earthquake and tsunami, with the science editor adding entire sections about earthquakes and tsunamis. Plus wait till you see the photographs! Some of yours are really very good and we were hoping that you would want us to use some of them in the issue."

"I'm speechless, Doris. Wow. You mean my photographs are good enough for the magazine's issues?"

"Well yes. We need a lot of photographs since we have to do the whole issue."

After Sophie read their stories, she made a few comments, which Doris liked and agreed to change some little things. Sophie added that she had some stories that the children told her when she was watching them at the army base. Sophie pointed to the photos she had of the children and told Doris the children's names and their stories. Doris asked her to write down some of the stories with the pictures of each child that she remembered. Later after Doris read Sophie's stories, she was impressed and said that she would be sending each photo of each child and their individual story to the editor. Sophie was cautiously optimistic that the magazine might actually use one of her photographs. She returned home to prepare for Tessa's wedding, with thoughts of her own future with Wayne.

CHAPTER THREE

It was a fairy tale wedding in St. Louis Cathedral, a dream that many young women would have longed for. It was more elaborate than Tessa wanted, but Geoff helped plan it and he kept going overboard with every detail. The bridesmaids dresses were rainbow colored with their flowers and the flowers decorating the church in the same designs. Sophie was her maid-of-honor and Tessa's little sister was the flower girl. The best man was Geoff's brother. The bridesmaids and groomsmen were friends and family of Tessa and Geoff. The cathedral was packed. Their friends and families took up only a third of the church as locals and tourists were overjoyed to be able to observe a fancy wedding in the French Quarter. The photographer was given instructions to take photos of the wedding party before and after the ceremony in Jackson Square in front of the cathedral. At least the weather cooperated so they could take the pictures outside as it had rained the day before. Geoff had also insisted that they hire the horse drawn carriages that were everywhere in the French Quarter, instead of limousines to take them to the reception. And that, of course, had to be at Antoines, one of the best and oldest restaurants in New Orleans. Tessa didn't realize Geoff had such exquisite tastes, but she figured that since he wanted to be a doctor, he deserved the best. Her parents were skeptical about the expense but thought that if Tessa wanted the best wedding, she should have it. They were not exactly enamored with Geoff, but didn't dislike him either. Tessa was never able to become friendly with his family as they were stand-offish. Geoff's father was a butcher and his mother worked at the local Elmers Candy factory, while Tessa's father had a good job at the University of New Orleans and her mother was able to stay home to raise her children.

Geoff had also hired a local Jazz Brass Band to follow the carriages to Antoines, and a different band to play at the reception. Food and drink flowed freely as their friends and family celebrated. The wedding cake was enormous and the grooms cake was shaped like a doctors bag with a real stethoscope coming out of it.

Their college friends ate, danced and drank until most of them were drunk. They were feeling the happiness of a wedding and celebrating their freedom as they entered into adulthood realizing that a chapter of their lives was over, one that was controlled and directed by parents and teachers. Their freedom was beginning and many of them were scared of the future but would never admit it. This was not yet the time for good-byes but in their minds they knew that this was going to be the last time they would be together as a group as some of them would be going out of town to further their education, or for a job out of town.

They danced to the music of *Blue Velvet, I Will Follow Him, Days of Wine and Roses, Our Day Will Come*, and many others. The band played overtime as many of the members were friends of theirs from the music school, especially Vic who played the piano. Vic could always be found in the student union entertaining everyone by playing requests on the piano as they all sang along. Although the band was taking a break, Vic stayed at the piano. It was as if no one wanted the reception to end. Soon Tessa was changing into her going-away clothes, then she and Geoff drove off to begin a new life.

It all happened so fast that Tessa couldn't believe it was over. Smiling in her reverie, she found herself driving through Atlanta on their way to a honeymoon in the Smoky Mountains. Tessa thought Geoff was sleeping in the passenger seat as she came to a construction site. She was confused as to which way to go and took a wrong turn. Geoff started yelling at her, "Where the hell are you going?"

"I don't know. The signs are all screwed up and I couldn't see which way to go." Tessa said as she looked scornfully at Geoff for yelling at her. "Look on the map and see where we are supposed to go."

"Pull over into that parking lot. I'm going to take over since you can't drive."

Tessa felt like crying. She didn't do anything wrong so why was Geoff so mad at her. "Maybe we should get something to eat. We've been driving for hours and I'm getting tired and hungry."

"Fine, I'm tired and hungry too. I think it's time for a break."

Tessa was relieved when Geoff cooled off. But she remembered a time after she met his family that he had gotten mad at his mother and threw something across the room at her. She couldn't remember why he was so mad but she dismissed it as his being upset over something. Then she started remembering other things that Geoff did that Tessa shrugged it off. There was the time when they were picking out their silver, china and glassware. Tessa showed Geoff the patterns that she chose, but he was not impressed. He said, "Is that what you like? That's ugly." The next day he went with her and chose more modern patterns. Tessa thought it looked fine so she accepted it and thought that maybe she didn't have that good of a taste anyway.

The rest of the honeymoon was without incident, but Tessa was beginning to feel uneasy. She felt that she had to be careful not to upset Geoff. *There's been so much excitement,* she thought, *Geoff getting accepted into medical school, graduation, the excitement of planing our wedding, getting an apartment near the school, moving, and me getting that job teaching, that when things calm down and we get into a routine and I start earning some money, everything will be great.*

Tessa had met Geoff in their sophomore year of college where they had a class together. He had transferred from another school and was not one of her and Sophie's friends that they grew up with. Tessa was not romantically interested in any of the men in their clique that they knew since childhood; they were more like brothers to her. Tessa didn't really have any ideas for her future, like most women, she thought she would get married and have a family and be content being someone's wife and mother. She wasn't all that interested in going to college, but that is what all of her friends did and there was nothing much else for a woman to do after high school if she was not going to get married right away. She wasn't that interested in majoring in teaching either, but there were no other classes she wanted to take. She was going along with her peers doing what she thought society expected of her with no real expectations except to find a man to share her life with. When Geoff walked into her class that day, he was so electrifying and vivacious, nothing like anyone she had ever met before. He had a presence that shouted out to everyone, "I am here." When he walked into a room, everyone paid attention. Everyone wanted to be his friend. His personality was the opposite of Tessa's. When Tessa walked into a classroom, she took a seat in the back corner so no one would notice her. She didn't like the attention, but admired those who demanded it. For Tessa, Geoff was everything she wasn't and thought she could never be. In her later years, Tessa wondered what he ever saw in her, except that she had a pliable personality and perhaps Geoff subconsciously thought he could mold her into whatever he wanted her to be. Tessa accepted that because she had no idea of what she was supposed to be anyway. She let life impose its will on her instead of willing herself to live.

They were set up in a small inexpensive apartment for medical students near the LSU Medical Center in New Orleans where Geoff was accepted. Tessa thought they would be spending the rest of the summer together before his classes started and her job teaching would begin, but Geoff had other plans. He spent most of his time away from home explaining that he wanted to get a head start with his studies and said he was at the school library or with other medical students learning what he could about what was expected of him. Tessa spent that time learning what to cook for him. Many nights he would come home late and tell her that he had already eaten. One night he was hungry and what Tessa had cooked was overdone. "What the hell is this?" he shouted. "I can't eat this crap. Don't you know how to cook?"

"You didn't tell me what time you were coming home, so I had to keep it warm. I never know what time you will be here. How am I supposed to have dinner ready when you don't even call to tell me when you will be here or if you already ate out?" Tessa was on the verge of tears again. Geoff left the apartment again slamming the door behind him. He didn't return home until the next night and acted as if nothing was the matter. Tessa didn't want to bring it up for fear of upsetting him again. *Things will get better when both of our schools start and we get into a routine,* she thought.

CHAPTER FOUR

"There's a package for you. It came in today's mail while you were out." Sophie's mother said.

Sophie unwrapped the copy of *The WorldView* that Doris sent her. It was the issue with her story and photographs. She felt a tingle down her spine as she saw the pages with her photographs and stories. She hugged her mother and they both had tears in their eyes. "I can't believe this! My story and photographs are in this national magazine. I'm just out of college, couldn't get a job at the *Times Picayune* but got my work into a national magazine. Do they really think I'm that good?"

"Sometimes those things just happen." her mother said. "You were in the right place at the right time, and you met the right people. Doris already called and will call again tonight, probably to congratulate you."

When the phone rang, Sophie assumed it would be Doris, but Wayne was calling. "We're all going out tomorrow night. I'll pick you up at 7:30." Sophie wanted to tell Wayne the news but didn't want to hang on the phone in case Doris was calling. So she didn't tell him anything about the magazine and cut the call short saying that she was very busy at the moment. When the phone rang next it was Doris.

"How does it feel to see you work in *The WorldView*?" Doris asked.

"It's unbelievable! I didn't think the editors would put my work in the magazine since I'm an amateur."

"They were quite impressed. They loved the take you had on the children. They were especially impressed with the way you wrote about the children in the village of Afognak. You wrote about their lives and then the tribute to them after they were lost in the tsunami was very touching. I think I saw tears in the eyes of the editors, which is an incredible feat for those seemingly hardened men. In fact besides calling to congratulate you, the real reason I'm calling is to invite you to accompany us on our next assignment."

"Are you serious?"

"Absolutely. We haven't found a replacement for Jack yet and since you were so helpful we would like you to join us again."

Sophie accepted without a thought about how Wayne would react, which was not pleasant when she told him. He almost broke off their engagement, but she reassured him that she would be back soon when the magazine hired someone permanently. She didn't think she was good enough to be writing for a famous popular magazine for very long. It was too exciting to pass up.

As time passed and Doris and Len kept asking her to accompany them on the next assignment, and the next, and the next, Sophie was caught up in the excitement of visiting so many places. They traveled to many countries in South America visiting the indigenous people there. After they wrote and photographed the villagers they had time to see many of the landmarks such as caves, waterfalls, and mountains. Sophie always wrote and photographed the children in all the places they went. Sophie began to wonder if they were ever going to hire someone else to replace Jack. She finally decided to ask Doris.

"You are doing wonderful work. I see improvement every time we finish an assignment. It would be a shame to let you go when you are learning so much. So the boss said we could keep you permanently, that is if you want the job."

"I don't know what to say. It has been an honor to work with you. Of course I would love this to be permanent"

Her decision to continue was also because her relationship with Wayne was deteriorating. Each time she returned home, Wayne was more and more distant. After a while, they stopped going out and only talked on the phone. Recently, when she tried to call him, he didn't even answer. His parents kept telling her that he was out. They said they would give him the message to call her, but he never did. On one of her latest trips home, Sophie found out through Tessa that he was seeing someone else, a friend who was always interested in him through college and later even while she was dating him. On a recent phone call home to her parents, they reluctantly told her that Wayne got married. Sophie was annoyed that Wayne couldn't tell her to her face. She was sad at losing Wayne, but thought it was for the better. Sophie was having so much fun and learning so much that she knew she would not have been happy giving it all up to be a wife and mother. She accepted that having this career was what she wanted more than living the dream that she and Tessa used to talk about. Eventually, she stopped thinking of Wayne and what they might have had.

PART TWO

CHAPTER FIVE

The street was wet after the sudden afternoon rain shower that usually occurred in the summer. She wasn't used to wearing heels and her calves started to ache. She rounded the corner by the Cathedral and headed toward Jackson Square. The thought hit her that this was the scene of her wedding almost ten years ago. She stopped abruptly as she looked around remembering the wedding pictures. She felt the tears welling up and thought, *I should turn around and go home. I can't let them see me like this.* But she did really want to see her old friends again. She was anxious as well as nervous and took a deep breath. She looked around again this time not trying to remember, but to take in the sights of the French Quarter; the artist doing a charcoal portrait of a pretty girl as the boyfriend watched, another artist drinking coffee by his paintings of local scenes, the old lady feeding crumbs to the pigeons, boys hurrying by on their skateboards, tourists milling about going in all different directions in their crisp colorful summer outfits looking at maps and pointing. After she felt that she had composed herself, she continued through Jackson Square. Her feet kept complaining as the shoes tightened around her feet. As she waited for the light to change, a carriage filled with tourists passed by, the horse looking tired and bored. She tried to put another thought out of her mind, the one of her in a wedding dress riding in a similar carriage towards her future. But the memories would not go away. She remembered when she was in that carriage, so happy going to her wedding and to a future that she thought was going to be as fantastic as the wedding. Her life after that was nothing like the dream she imagined. It became a nightmare she couldn't wake up from.

After they settled into a routine of Geoff going to his classes and her teaching first grade at a Catholic school, she thought Geoff would calm down and not yell at her like he did from the honeymoon on. But it only got worse. Geoff usually stayed out until late saying that he was studying, and sometimes didn't come home at all. She never knew if she should have a good meal fixed or not. When she did, he sometimes didn't come home, and when she didn't, he would come home angry at having nothing to eat. Soon after they settled into their apartment, he would occasionally find something to argue with her about, but what that was she could no longer remember. Eventually it got to where he would push her down and go to bed mad. Then the pushing got stronger as the months went by until he would violently knock her down and she would fall onto furniture and have bruises the next day. One day he began hitting her. Mostly he would hit her in the arms and she would have to wear long sleeves to work to hide the bruises. Sometimes he would knock her to the floor and get on top of her and scream at her how stupid she was. But Tessa kept making excuses to herself saying that Geoff was under a lot of pressure studying to become a doctor. She reasoned that things would get better once the semester was over, or the year was over or when

Geoff would finally become a doctor. But she knew deep down inside that his abusive behavior would never end. She realized this when the first baby was born.

In the second year of her marriage she discovered that she was pregnant. She thought surely this would be the cause of him not hitting her anymore. But it didn't. He took the news nonchalantly as if it didn't really matter to him that he was going to be a father. He didn't change in the least. But she did change. She was tired all the time, trying to hide the bruises and tears, having to go to work pregnant and always worried about what she would find when she got home. She worried that she would have to quit work and they would have no money coming in. Her school let her stay since the baby was due in the middle of summer and she didn't begin to show until the school year was almost over, so she was able to work until the end of the semester. She could go back for the next year, but had to find a day care center to put the baby in. Geoff told her there was no way she could stay home to care for the baby. She had to earn money so he could continue school. She hated bringing the baby to daycare, crying every day when she left him. Her life was spiraling downward, but she had to keep herself together for the baby's sake. She felt trapped in a life she never thought would happen. She felt there was nowhere to turn, no one to talk to, no way out.

When the baby was two years old, she was pregnant again. Geoff would sometimes apologize after his anger subsided and have sex with her. She didn't want sex with him anymore, but didn't dare object for fear of angering him again.

One day she heard some other teachers discussing someone's divorce. She never thought of divorce before since she was a Catholic and working in a Catholic school. Her idea of a Catholic marriage was "till death do us part." Soon the idea of divorce began growing in her mind. By that time, they had two sons, Geoff had become a doctor and they had moved into a new house. Geoff had picked it out without her input. She didn't even know he was house hunting or get to see it before he told her they were moving. He had just started earning a salary working in a local hospital. She asked if she could quit working and be home for their two sons, but he said no, there were still too many expenses. He had a student loan to pay back, and the new house note would eat up most of his salary and the expensive furniture he bought to fill it. He always had to have new expensive clothes and jewelry since he was now a doctor. Then of course he had to have a new BMW while she drove an old used Volkswagen Beetle. He had to maintain his image. The odd part was that in public, he seemed the perfect gentleman. No one suspected he had a violent side. Everyone thought he was a wonderful person.

There were times when Tessa tried to explain that the cost of putting both boys in daycare cost more than her salary as a teacher, therefore they were losing money, but Geoff didn't listen. He never listened to her. Eventually she stopped trying to discuss anything with him because every decision was his with no input from her. Any input she ever tried to give was dismissed by him as being stupid or wrong. So she learned to keep her mouth shut and tried not to antagonize him. This was what her life had become. She hated it and began to hate Geoff.

She began to lose faith in her religion too. She had stopped going to church on Sunday because she was so physically tired after working all week, and emotionally tired living with a time bomb every day. Without his knowledge, she went on birth control pills. Geoff didn't know, but Tessa figured he didn't care much about what she did anyway. Even though it was against her religion, she just didn't care anymore.

When her oldest boy was old enough to go to first grade, she was going to put him in the Catholic school where she worked. The principal had told her that would be ok. But when the school year was about to start and she went to get the paperwork, the principal told her there was no room for her son because they had to take in the neighborhood children first. This time Tessa got really angry, probably for the first time in her life. She felt betrayed after giving so much to the school and getting so little pay for it. Perhaps since she could not take her anger out at Geoff, she took it out on the first thing that she had some control of. She went immediately to the public school system to apply for a job there. They hired her right away since she had experience, but had to start in a low ranking school across the river, but to her pleasure, her salary was double what it was before. Then to get even with the Catholic school that had angered her, she didn't tell them she was quitting until the very first day of school. The fact that the nuns treated her so badly was another nail in the coffin of her beliefs.

The idea of divorce was growing in her mind also. It came to a head recently when Geoff got so mad that he knocked her down into the brick fireplace. She must have lost consciousness, because she woke up in the hospital. Geoff must have called an ambulance. Tessa had a memory loss about the incident at first, but when it came back to her what had happened, she was frightened. She began to think, *What if I had a severe brain injury, or I could have even died? Who would take care of my children? I can't let this go on. I'm going to get a divorce. But how will I live? I don't know how to be on my own.*

She decided to get advice from the local parish priest. When she went to see him and told him of all that had happened, he merely nodded his head as if in agreement. Then he dropped a bombshell on her that she would never forget. This priest who was supposed to be helpful told her flatly, "Wives must be submissive to their husbands." Tessa could not believe what he was telling her, that she must remain married to someone who was getting so abusive that she might end up beaten to death, and she was supposed to "bow down" to him? That's when she lost faith completely. How could this "Man of God" tell her she had to remain with a husband who might eventually seriously hurt or worse, kill her? How could this "Man of God" believe that's what God intended when he said "Till Death Do Us Part." Was she supposed to die for faith? No! She could not, would not believe that's what God and religion was supposed to be about. Never again would she set foot into a church. The seeds of cynicism were sewn along with those of agnosticism.

She knew also that asking for a divorce was not going to be easy. Naturally Geoff was angry and said that would never happen. Then he got into one of his rages and she ended up calling the police. They convinced Geoff that he ought to get out of the house for a while. He did moved out but said it was only going to be temporary. He went to live with his mother but came back into the house as he pleased saying it was his house and he had a right to be there. He tried to reason with her that a divorce would be detrimental to his career and hers, but she didn't believe that. She knew by then that that was his attempt to control the situation. He even tried to convince her that since she was over 30, divorced and with two children, she would never find a man who would want her. She began to understand how manipulative he was.

She became friendly with the school counselor and soon was revealing to her that she was not very happy in her marriage. Her friend suggested that she go to a psychologist. Tessa thought she couldn't afford that, but the friend mentioned a program at a local medical center that charged on a sliding scale. Tessa felt so desperate that she agreed to make an appointment. After a number of sessions, Tessa became more assertive and sure of herself. Still afraid of Geoff's temper, she felt she had to get out of the relationship no matter what the cost. She began divorce proceedings. It was a long and difficult procedure, Geoff trying at every opportunity to get her to change her mind, using every manipulative technique he had, but Tessa would not give in. Even after they were living apart, Geoff could still make her life difficult. Even so, Tessa felt better off not having to deal with him every day.

As she was thinking about her past, she was getting closer to the reunion, she almost lost her nerve again, but the light changed and tourists pushed her towards the corner. She took another deep breath, the odors of horse manure making her gag. *If only I were a tourist visiting some strange and exotic place,* she thought. *If only I could be like Sophie, traveling the world. We were so much alike, what happened that she ended up with such a wonderful life and me with a nightmare?*

Café Du Monde was crowded. She searched around for a recognizable face as she glanced around the tables. *Would I recognize anyone? Would they recognize me?* She didn't think that she had changed much over the years, but time has its own way of slowly altering things so as not to be noticed. She hadn't seen anyone much in the past ten years, only an occasional phone call and some post cards and letters from Sophie. How she envied Sophie, whose job was taking her all over the world. Sophie was free and happy and seemed to enjoy her life as a journalist. But Sophie never married. Wayne broke up with her after she kept going on one assignment after another, and was officially hired on to work with her friends, Doris and Len. Tessa wondered if Sophie regretted not getting married and having children. She wondered if it would be intrusive ask her.

Through the haze of powdered sugar permeating the air, Tessa spotted a table with a few women sitting there. After a closer look she recognized Sophie, although Sophie looked so sophisticated. They spotted Tessa and waved her over. *Well it's done now. They see me so I can't back out.* Tessa gathered up her courage and made her way over to the table trying to put on a smile. After the hugs and the look-how-great-you-look comments she sat down and ordered café au lait and beignets.

Amid the drone of the other conversations and the clanking of coffee mugs, they began relating their accounts of the years since graduation.

Everyone talked about their husbands, how great they were, and their children, how wonderful they were doing in school. Tessa showed them her family pictures and how her husband was doing well as a doctor and how they bought a new house in Old Metairie, a prestigious place to live. She smiled and commented on everyone's wonderful lives and avoided saying much more about her own. She wondered if they could see the sadness in her eyes as she talked about her life. She couldn't tell them how cruel her husband was and how she was divorcing him. She couldn't tell them how she hates her job and never thought she would have to work so long. She didn't want to talk about how she cried all the time and felt trapped. She wondered if their lives were as great as they recounted, or if they were leaving out all the negatives like she was doing. She looked around the table and thought *Are they as happy as they let on to be? Are they hiding the worst part of their lives like I am?*

After quickly talking about her children, she diverted the subject to Sophie. "Tell us about yourself. You are traveling all over the world. Where have you gone and what are you doing? You wrote to me about an award you received last year. Tell us about that."

Sophie began to tell them about the assignments she went on after the Alaskan adventure. She told them that Doris and Len had asked her to go with them to the next assignment, and then the next since they had not hired anyone else until she realized that they were not even looking anymore. Doris confirmed her thoughts when she told Sophie that she was good enough to remain their third person and could travel with them as long as she wanted to. Sophie was overjoyed as she was learning how to be an expert Journalist. Soon she stopped thinking about going back home to a normal life, getting married. Each time Sophie came home, she went out with Wayne, and each time Wayne was more distant until the time he didn't even answer her call. He had stopped talking about them getting married and their visits were getting shorter and shorter. Sophie found out after the last time she saw him that he was dating one of their friends from college who always had a crush on him. That was when they decided to officially break their engagement. A few years ago she found out that they had married and had a child. Putting the past behind her, she then put all of her efforts into her Journalism. She went on assignments with a new purpose, that of becoming a better journalist and learning more from Doris and Len each time. Everywhere she went she took photos of and wrote stories about the children. It started to be her speciality, writing the children's take on the events they were assigned to. After a few years of collecting the photos of the children, Doris told her she ought to publish a book of them. Sophie had kept notes and stories on most of the children she photographed. Sophie thought that might be a good idea, but didn't think it would be a great seller. But with Doris' help, Sophie wrote it. She opened the book with the children who lost their lives in the tsunami in her first assignment with Doris and Len. Many of the photos were heartbreaking knowing that these children would never grow up, never live their lives as teenagers and adults, never have families of their own.

Sophie chose the cover with a favorite photo of

hers of two children sleeping. It was a funny but sad picture. Eventually it became an award winning photo just as her book was. She told her friends of the time that the photo was taken.

"It was an amazingly busy summer. We had just finished an assignment covering the launch of the moon landing, then there was Hurricane Camille on the Gulf Coast. It seemed that we had been on a fast pace with so much happening, so we wanted to take a break. We were each going to go home for a while when Doris got a call from the editor about a group of people arranging a free concert in an open field. We thought we needed some fun down time so we told him we would go to see what that was all about. We wandered around amazed at how many people were there and how they were dressed and how they didn't have a care in the world. There were the signs, 'Make Love Not War' all over, and that's exactly what many of them were doing. It turned out to be Woodstock. It was a strange and funny experience. The photograph I took was of two children that I found sleeping amid all the noise and confusion. They had flowers all over them as they slept and it was the most adorable picture, and sad because they were so dirty. The dirt and the flowers were such a contrast and so typical of children. They were sleeping so soundly, oblivious to the loud music and dancing going on around them."

"You were at Woodstock?" one of the girls said.

"Yes and that's not all. As we were wandering around, the smell of pot was so strong everywhere that I got high. I had never smoked pot before and was feeling wonderful until I got so sick later that Doris and Len had to carry me back to the motel. They were so concerned about me but were laughing like I had never seen them laugh before. I think they were a little high too. I always thought you had to smoke it to get high, but there was so much, the air was thick with the smell, and I guess it permeated our skin."

The friends laughed as Sophie continued her story. "As Doris was helping me arrange the book, we thought of publishing it with the proceeds going to a children's fund." Sophie wasn't interested in making money from the book as she was doing well enough, so she offered to donate all of the proceeds to the Organization for Children. The company that published *The WorldView* was interested and agreed to publish her book.

The book was well accepted throughout the world and made a fortune for the children's fund. It was for this that Sophie was given a special award. She recounted to her friends the awards banquet in Chicago where all of the big publishing companies attended. Almost all of the CEO's were there. Sophie asked Doris to point out who was CEO of each publishing company, especially the one for Hawthorne Publishing Company who was the publisher for *The WorldView,* who was technically her boss. He was sitting a few tables away from them, and gave a nod and a wave to their table when he saw that Doris was pointing him out to Sophie. Sophie smiled and waved back to him. Sophie thought it was a little odd that her award was given to her by the CEO of a rival company. She assumed that it was because the CEO of Hawthorne was in a wheelchair and didn't want to go up to the podium.

It was getting late and their friends excused themselves because they had to return home to cook for their families. Sophie said that she was going to take the streetcar home but Tessa offered her a ride. "That would be great, thanks," Sophie accepted. "If you have time you could come in and say hello to my parents."

"I'd like that," Tessa answered. "I haven't seen them in years. Even though I live here, I feel bad that I haven't spoken to them in so long." Tessa decided that she should tell Sophie that she had just divorced Geoff. She felt she could talk to Sophie better than the other girls since they used to be such close friends. Tessa started to tell Sophie about it, but not the reasons or the worst parts of it, just that they did not get along anymore and Tessa was unhappy. She told Sophie that Geoff was very manipulative and wanted to control everything.

"I'm sorry." said Sophie. "I didn't know you were having problems. You both seemed to be the perfect couple."

"I just couldn't tell anyone. I feel so bad. It's like I'm the only one of our group that doesn't have a wonderful life. You heard the others how happy and settled they all are. I feel as if I failed somehow."

"No Tessa, no. It's not your fault. It seems that Geoff was not what you thought he was and that's not what you wanted in a marriage."

"Yes that's exactly what my therapist tells me, that it's not my fault."

"You are seeing a therapist? I think that's a great idea." Sophie replied.

"I sort of feel like seeing a therapist is admitting that there is something wrong with me. Only really sick people see a therapist."

"No, not at all, not anymore. Everyone needs to be able to talk openly to someone, and I'm sorry I could not be here for you. And anyway, more and more people are going to see a therapist."

"Oh, don't apologize for not being there for me, Sophie. You have you own life and career and I don't want to spoil it with my problems."

"You are not spoiling anything. You can talk to me, after all we are friends and that's what friends are for."

"Thank you for that. I don't want your parents to know any of this just yet. Let's just have a pleasant visit."

"Ok, well here we are. Do you have time to come in and say hello to my parents?"

"Yes, of course."

As they entered Sophie's house, Sophie called out, "Mom! Dad! Look who's here! Tessa came to see you."

There was no answer. Sophie went all throughout the house and looked out the back door, but didn't see her parents anywhere. Sophie was not yet alarmed until Tessa found a note on the kitchen table. "Look, Sophie, they left you a note. Maybe they went out with friends."

Sophie opened the note and paled. "Oh no. My mother wrote that they went to the hospital. She said that my father had a heart attack and they called for an ambulance. I have to go there right away. Tessa can you drive me to the hospital?"

"Yes, of course, Let's go"

When they reached the hospital, Tessa asked, "Do you want me to come in with you?"

"No, it's ok. You go on home to your boys. I'm sure Dad will be fine."

"Ok, call me and let me know how he is doing."

Sophie found her mother in a sitting room

near the emergency room. She had her head in her hands and Sophie could tell that she was crying.

"Mom, what happened? Where's Dad? Is he Ok?"

"He's gone, Sophie. He's gone."

"What do you mean he's gone? Your note said that he had a heart attack. He can't be gone."

"It was a massive attack and they couldn't save him." her mother cried. "He died in the ambulance. They couldn't revive him. He was gone before they reached the hospital. The doctors did all they could, but it was too late."

Tessa left Sophie at the hospital, not knowing what had happened to her friend's father. She was still thinking of how she wanted to confide in Sophie about her problems, but with Sophie's tragedy, she did not get the chance to talk more to her friend. Tessa did not want to return home just yet. Her mother was watching the boys for the weekend. She ended up driving out to the lakefront. She sat on the steps by the lake and watched the sailboats. Tears fell down her cheeks as she thought of the fun those people were having out on their boats on a beautiful Saturday. She wondered why her life had turned out to be so terrible. All she ever wanted was to be married to a nice man and have a family she could be proud of. Instead she ended up with an abusive husband and working in a job she despised with no idea of how to realize her dreams, not even knowing what those dreams were anymore. She knew that the divorce was inevitable. She could not stay in a situation that was causing her so much pain. She would go back Monday to her lawyer to see what was going to happen next. She wiped away her tears and aimlessly drove around the city. When she got to her mother's house to pick up her boys, there was a message that Sophie had called with bad news. Sophie's father had died.

The funeral arrangements were made. There would be a wake Monday night and a church service and burial on Tuesday. A few of their friends who were still in town attended the services. Sophie was surprised to see Wayne there. He gave her his condolences as he hugged her tightly. Even though his wife was one of their friends from college, she did not attend. Sophie was surprised to see how much older he looked. He apologized for not being able to stay longer and left. As she watched him leave, she wondered what might have been if she had married him. She thought how strange life is, thinking that it is going to be one way, but unexpected things happen and everything changes. Once again, she felt the realities of life, death, and loss.

After the funeral, she stayed with her mother for a couple of months until her mother convinced her she would be fine and for Sophie to go on to her next assignment with Doris and Len. But this was to be the last assignment they would go on together. When Sophie received the award, she was offered many positions at numerous popular magazines. One children's magazine wanted her as the assistant editor. She considered that position, but was reluctant to leave Doris. During their travels on the assignment, Doris told Sophie that she was getting too tired to continue traveling and wanted to retire, so Sophie would be free to take another position at any magazine she wanted. Sophie had noticed that Doris was not her usual self the last couple of years.

CHAPTER SIX

The retirement dinner for Doris was well attended by many important people in the magazine and publishing business. Doris's close friend, Marge, payed close attention to Doris, hovering over her like a mother hen. Sophie was going over to talk to Doris when she saw Doris and Marge sitting at a table having an intimate conversation. It was when Sophie saw them holding hands under the table that she realized Doris and Marge were more than close friends. They were lovers. Sophie stopped in her tracks. She was visibly pale. She knew that Doris and Marge lived together when they were not on assignment, but only realized their relationship at the retirement dinner. Sophie didn't know if she should be horrified or pleased. She had never known anyone who was gay before, and didn't know how to react. Her innocent upbringing didn't prepare her for this sort of thing even though she and Doris were close throughout their years of working together, Doris did not share this part of her life with Sophie. They had been to a few parties together and she had met Marge before, but didn't realize what their relationship was until this moment at the retirement dinner. Doris must have seen Sophie's reaction because she went over to Sophie and told her, "I'm sorry Sophie, I thought you knew. I should have realized that you never thought of Marge and me as a couple."

"Oh, Doris. I must have been so self absorbed in my own happiness about my career that I didn't give much thought to other people's private lives."

"For as much as you've learned the past few years, you still have a lot to learn about life."

"I guess you're right, Doris. Wow. I feel so clueless. So much has happened to me that I didn't expect. I'm living in a dream world and I'm afraid that I'll wake up to a normal and boring life anytime now. This world has so many surprises and twists and turns, that I feel I'll never understand it all."

"You're young and resilient. You have a long way to go yet. Anytime you want to talk, just come by and visit. I hope you won't forget me."

"Of course I won't forget you. How can you say that? I'll come visit all the time. I suppose I still have a lot to learn from you. I am really happy for you." As they hugged each other, Sophie realized how frail Doris had become. Sophie knew that Doris was a lot older, but wondered if she was ill. But Doris told her that she was just tired and through years of bad habits, like smoking and drinking too much sometimes, she was feeling the effects of aging, and wanted to spend more time relaxing.

Sophie soon settled in to her new position at the children's magazine. She was hired along with other young people to remake the image of the magazine as readership was declining. After a few months of meetings and sessions, Sophie came up with an idea. She explained at the meetings that since the magazine was aimed at the middle school age child, they ought to devote each monthly issue to a specific state. Others liked the idea and had more suggestions as to what ought to be included, such as what would interest children of that age to visit more of their state. Someone suggested adding a teacher's page with ideas for lesson plans. With an entire issue devoted to each state, that would give the magazine more than four years of issues, and would increase the orders from schools across the country. After deciding to present the issues alphabetically by state, the teams of writers and photographers would then spend weeks in each state looking for items of interest. Sophie wanted to be part of the visiting teams.

It was over two years before Louisiana was chosen for a future issue. She was anxious to return home to visit her mother and friends. She had been visiting her mother for short periods during holidays, but didn't connect with her friends except for postcards and short phone calls. She was worried about her mother since her father died. She noticed her mother getting more forgetful and wondered if she should be there more often, or move her mother to New York to live with her. Her mother rejected the idea of moving saying that this was her home and she wasn't going to leave.

By the time Sophie went home to research Louisiana for the magazine, her mother seemed to be worse. It was when her mother had a minor automobile accident that Sophie thought it was time to take her driving privileges away. She convinced her mother that it would save a lot of expenses of owning a car, and that she could take a taxi to places she needed to go, but Sophie worried what would happen when she had to return to New York, leaving her mother alone. Her mother had a few friends, but they were no better off as they were about the same age and in the same condition as her mother.

While in New Orleans, Sophie arranged another reunion with her friends from college. It had been over five years since her father died. That was also the last time she had met her friends at Cafè Du Monde, and she didn't know much about their lives since then. Everyone wanted to get together, but her closest friend, Tessa, was the only one who was able to meet with her this time. Their other college friends were too busy wrapped up in their lives with family and other friends.

Tessa picked up Sophie one Sunday to go to Brennan's in the French Quarter for brunch. They made small talk during the meal, then went to Tessa's house. Sophie was surprised to learn that Tessa didn't live in Old Metairie anymore even though she knew that Geoff had died. She thought Tessa was able to keep the house, but instead she lived in an apartment by the lake near the University of New Orleans.

Tessa started to explain what had happened to her life since their last reunion.

"Geoff and I had gotten a divorce. He was nothing like what I thought when we met in class. My life with him was getting progressively worse. He became abusive until I couldn't take it anymore."

"Oh, Tessa, I'm so sorry. Why didn't you tell me this before."

"At first, I was ashamed. I didn't think there was anyone else who was abused like I was. But as the years went by, and through my therapy, I learned that this is a huge problem. There were no places for me, or anyone like me to get help. Even the priest at the church told me I had to stay with him because we were married and they didn't allow divorces."

"Is that why you don't go to church anymore?"

"That's part of it. But there are many more reasons. Geoff's family seemed to be very religious and went to church regularly, and after Geoff died I discovered how evil they really were. After his funeral, they didn't want anything to do with me or my sons. I felt like an outcast, even though I was never really close to his family. I don't think they ever liked me. I never spoke to them again."

"What happened?" Sophie asked.

"They blamed me for his death. But even that is no reason to disown my sons."

"How did they think his death was your fault?"

"When Geoff was going to medical school, he started taking pills. At first it was to stay awake to study, then it was to get some sleep. He was hardly ever home, so I didn't know what he was doing. When he got the job at the hospital, he continued to take pills. Then it became easier to get the pills from the drug store in the hospital. He would order pills for patients and take one or two out of the order. I didn't find out about any of this until after his death when one of his doctor friends told me. I don't know if the drugs made him abusive or not, but when he did come home, he got mad at any little thing I did. When I divorced him, he got worse, blaming me for anything that was wrong with him. He wouldn't leave me alone and kept coming to the house saying it was his and he could do as he pleased. Eventually, he became unable to work because he was so drugged up. When the hospital realized he was stealing the drugs, and saw how he was, they fired him. It was just a few months later that he was found dead in a motel room on Airline Highway with pills and liquor in the room."

"Who found him?"

"Apparently, he was there with a hooker. She left the room and called 911 anonymously. They never found out who she was, but the police said that he was frequently seen at that motel with hookers."

"That's awful. You never knew what he was doing, but his family blamed you for his problems."

"Yes. They told someone that I was responsible, I was not a good wife, that it was my fault he took drugs and had to be with hookers. But the story gets worse. He left me with nothing. I should say less than nothing. He had somehow borrowed on the house to pay for his habits. I don't know how he did it, but he took out a second mortgage forging my name on it, so I owed more on the house than it was worth. Then more bills kept coming in and with my salary, I couldn't pay them. I had to declare bankruptcy, and the bank took the house. When I tried calling his family for a little help for the boys, they refused to talk to me unless it was to call me every name in the book."

"But why did they do that to the children?"

"I'm not really sure, but I think it's because Geoff's parents grew up in the ninth ward and I seemed to them to be from a sophisticated family. His father was friendly enough with me but I could never get close to his mother. I felt like she looked down her nose at me. I heard that they even questioned if Geoff was the father to our boys.

"Maybe she was jealous of you, because you took away her first born son."

"She was always distant, so maybe you're right. She had to work to help with the expenses, especially to send Geoff to college His father was a butcher and they lived in a small house in Gentilly. After Hurricane Betsy, they lost everything. Geoff couldn't help them because he was just starting medical school. I think they resented the fact that my parents didn't have to go through the problems that his parents did. Therapy helped me to see that there are people who resent others because they don't have the ambition to rise up above their own situation. They seem to expect other people to give them what they need. They feel that they are privileged and society owes them something for their sufferings."

"That's a shame. You should have called me. I would have helped you."

"I know you would have, but it was my problem and as I said, I was too embarrassed. How could I tell anyone what was going on. I could hardly face my coworkers. After Geoff died I asked for a transfer to another school. But I knew that even those teachers knew what had happened."

"I would have thought that you would have found some strength in going to church."

"No. Quite the opposite. No one there ever helped me. I guess I became so cynical and unhappy that I stopped believing in anything. I even blamed myself for a while, thinking that I must have done something wrong. But therapy has helped me a lot through the years. It was when I really hit bottom, I cried all the time, could barely face going to work every day, when one of my teacher friends told me about her therapist. So I began to see a different therapist and over the last few years, he helped me to realize that what Geoff did was not my fault and there was probably nothing I could have done to change things. So I put the past aside and am moving on with my life."

"I'm glad you are doing better. You seem to be stronger now. I would have helped you, you only had to ask."

"My strength comes from realizing that I didn't give up. I found out that I can do things I never thought I could do before. I always thought that my goal was to be married, have a nice family, and I would be taken care of forever. I never expected that I would have to work for a living. I never wanted a career. You remember how we used to think the only choice we had back then was to have a family? How times have changed. Neither one of us ended up having that dream realized. Do you ever regret not marrying Wayne?" Tessa asked.

"I think about that sometimes. I can't say how it would have turned out, but I am happy with what I have become. I love my work. I've traveled all over the world and met people I never would have met. I can't say how I would have been if I didn't have the chance to do what I am doing today. I think I knew at some point that I couldn't have Wayne wait for me, so when I found out that he was seeing someone else, I was kind of relieved that I was free to continue what I was doing and not have to feel guilty that he was waiting for me. In a sense, he took away the fact that I would have to choose between him and my career. I'm not sure I would have chosen him. I'm not sure that I ever loved him that much. When the opportunity came along to work for the magazine, I knew that I had to see what that kind of life was all about. It seems that things just fell into place."

"I'm not sure that I loved Geoff that much either. It was for me, that was the only choice I had. I think I fell in love with the idea of being in love and having a happy marriage. Anyway, what did I know then? I was just a naïve teenager doing what society expected."

"What are you doing now?"

"I realized I needed to make more money if I was the sole support of my boys, so I went back to school in the evenings and got a masters degree in teaching. I never really wanted to be a teacher and didn't enjoy it, but I learned how to be a good one. It worked out for the best since I had the same time off as my boys."

"How are they doing?" asked Sophie.

"They went through a bad time for a while after Geoff died. They had a hard time accepting that their own family rejected them. But they are better now. They understand that there are people in the world who are so narcissistic that no one else matters to them. They realize that Geoff and his whole family are like that."

"Then everything is going well for you?"

"I'm not really happy. I'm just in a comfortable place for now."

"You don't seem to be as cynical as before. Are you going back to church?"

"No. I don't believe in religion anymore. I'm still cynical, maybe even more so. I guess I just don't show it like I used to."

"But you are over the trauma of Geoff?"

"Very much so. I don't think of him much anymore. I treat it like a bad movie that I once saw and can put it out of my mind. In fact, I started dating after Geoff died."

"Are you dating someone now?"

"No. But I had met someone that I thought I could really love. He was so kind and caring and attentive. I was really falling in love."

"Are you with him now."

"No. We dated for almost two years, mostly we saw each other when my boys were spending the weekend at my parents house. Towards the end of the two years, we didn't see each other as much and I became worried. I confronted him one day as we were driving around and the song, *Torn Between Two Lovers* came on the radio. I wanted to change the station but he stopped me. The way he looked at me then, I suddenly knew. He was seeing someone else. We talked about it and he told me that he really did love me, but could not accept having to be a stepfather. He never wanted children. He married the other girl and as far as I know, they didn't have children."

"Tessa, you've really had a hard time in life, haven't you. No wonder you are so cynical. I don't know how I would have handled it after so many let-downs. I don't think I could have."

"I didn't handle it well at first. I was so depressed, devastated, and sick. I thought my life was getting better when I started dating, but then got another blow when I was really in love and he left me. My therapist told me I needed to find some outlet to take my mind off of my pain. We discussed some things I could do, then he told me about a clinic for battered women that was opening up and needed people to help out. He always said that no matter how bad I thought my life was, there were many more people worse off than me. He told me to try to find something to be grateful for every day. I thought it was a stupid idea and couldn't think of anything. But he kept at it until I agreed to try. He told me that since I knew about how battered women were treated and how they felt trapped, I should go to the clinic just to see what it was all about. So I started going there to see what I could do. I spend a lot of my time there now. It has brought me some measure of peace, thinking that I can help other women who are going through what I went through, letting them know that there is a way out and they don't have to remain in a bad situation. I think I have found a sense of meaning to my life. Remember when we thought all there was for us was to be married and someone's wife and mother? That was all we thought our future was to be. But there is much more than that. We can do something that makes a difference for others."

"Yes, I remember thinking that way. Many people still think that 'A woman's place is in the home,' but so many women are proving that that is not the case."

"You are a great example of that, Sophie. Look how much you have done. You have a career and you travel all over the world. If you had married Wayne, you wouldn't have been able to do that. Did you know that he is the assistant manager at the bank now?"

"I didn't know that. I'm glad he's doing well."

"What's next for you? Where are you going next?"

"Working for this children's magazine, I mostly go to a different state each month, and I'm here because the next issue is about Louisiana, but I'm thinking of taking time off to stay here a while. Since my father passed away, my mother is not doing well. She is forgetting a lot lately and I have been finding her just staring out the window. When I call to her she seems like she doesn't hear me, or is in some kind of trance. I'm worried about her. I'm going to go with her to her next doctor's visit to see what he thinks."

The Doctor had bad news. He told Sophie that her mother was suffering from Alzheimer's disease and it was not a good idea for her to live alone, as she was only going to get worse. There was evidence that she had suffered from small strokes, hardly noticeable but they showed up on the brain scan. Sophie had a life changing decision to make. She considered her options. She could move her mother to New York, hire someone to stay with her either here or in New York, put her mother in a home, or Sophie could quit working and move back to care for her. Sophie called the magazine and told them she needed some time off to figure out what was best for her mother.

Sophie remained with her mother for a few months, but realized that as her mother's health was declining, Sophie was not equipped to take care of her properly. It was the day that Sophie had gone to the grocery thinking it would not be a problem to leave her mother alone for a while, but when she returned, her mother was nowhere in sight. Frantic, she called 911. Eventually, her mother was found wandering around Audubon Park, still in her night gown. Sophie knew then that she would have to put her mother in a home where she would get round the clock attention. Sadly, she and the doctor arranged for her mother to be put in a comfortable home near the lake.

Sophie visited her mother every day, but each day her mother recognized Sophie less and less. The doctor informed Sophie that she needed to get on with her life, that her mother would be well taken care of. Sophie wandered around her house going from room to room remembering the good times she had growing up. Even though she was an only child, Sophie was never lonely. Her parents had taken her to most of the local attractions: Audubon Park and Zoo, Pontchartrain Beach, famous restaurants along the lake and in the French Quarter, City Park, and to the Mardi Gras parades. Her parents often let her friends accompany them, even when they went to the Gulf Coast in Mississippi and Florida for summer vacations. Her friend, Tessa, was the one who went almost everywhere with them. Tessa was as close as two sisters could be. Sophie called Tessa. She told Tessa everything that had happened with her mother and asked Tessa to come over.

"I know this is hard for you," said Tessa, "but you need to go through the house and decide what you want to do with your mother's things."

"I know I should do that, but it is like letting go of her while she is still here. I know she will never come back here. I looked around the other day and saw that she never let go of my father's things. All of his stuff is still where he left it. I thought she had accepted his death, but I think now that she never got over it. I should have come home more often."

"There is nothing you could have done. You couldn't give up your life just to be here with your mother. She wouldn't have wanted that. That's probably why she told you she was doing fine."

"Yes, I just need some time to accept what is happening. We go on with our lives as if nothing is going to change, but the changes creep up on us until one day we realize that our lives are so different than what we had planned. Look at us. Is this what we thought we would be doing when we were carefree youths in college wondering what we would be doing in the future? We thought we would get married, and raise a family. I never pictured that I would have to care for my mother."

"Neither one of us ended up how we thought we would. What happened? We thought we were following our plans, but some unforeseen force changed us. Do you think we were destined to do what we did? Did things happen to us that were supposed to happen?"

"Oh, you mean like fate. Are we where we are supposed to be, or could we have done something differently? If we had known the outcome, would we have changed anything?" Sophie mused.

"Who knows. But we have to go on from here no matter what. Looking back gets you nowhere, since you can't change what has already happened. That's what I do. I hardly ever think about the past. It's too depressing. It's something that happened to someone else, someone I choose not to be anymore. I don't plan for the distant future either. I just take things as they come and let what happens next happen. But we still have a choice. We are both still free to decide our next move. I can continue working at the battered women's clinic, or not. I choose to work there because I feel I am helping others, maybe making a difference for someone else, letting them know they don't have to accept things the way they are, that there is a better future for them if they choose to get out of their bad relationship."

"You are working for a better future for yourself, too. You are in a much better place now than you were a few years ago. I feel as if I am at a crossroad now. I don't know where to go next or what to do. Should I stay here or should I go back to work for the magazine? I don't know what to do next."

"I think you should clean out the attic. Remember when we went up there and found those papers about someone named Phillip? Did you ever ask your parents about him, or find out who he was?"

"No, I never asked them. It never seemed like the right time. Now neither of my parents can answer that question."

"Then that should be your next step. See what you can find out by looking through your parents papers. Besides, you might need to find insurance documents, or papers on the ownership of this house, stuff you're going to need, since your mother can't tell you anything anymore. I don't mean to sound heartless, but that's reality."

"Do you want to go up there and help me?" Sophie asked her friend. "Like we did such a long time ago?"

"No. I think that is something you need to do on your own. I'm going to have to go back to the clinic soon. Why don't we end on a positive note and go have lunch at Brennan's like we did years ago?"

The next day, Sophie went into the attic and brought down the strong box that contained the papers about Phillip. She felt a little guilty going through her parent's things, but knew that they could not object. She suddenly had a strong feeling that she had to know more. Who was Phillip? Why didn't her parents tell her anything about him? Why didn't she ever ask them? There was the birth and death certificate again. It was the same birthday as hers. How could this be? If he was her twin, why didn't it say so? The two certificates had a slightly different look. She couldn't pinpoint exactly what the difference was, it was so subtle. She put them aside and continued looking through the strong box to see what else was in there. Way in the back was a book. Curious. It was in French. It was called *Le Petit Prince.* Why would there be a French book in here? Whose was it? Was it her mother's or father's book? They never mentioned that they had French heritage. Sophie carefully examined the book. She found that she could read and understand the story. She had taken one French course in High School and found it was easy, but didn't pursue it any further. As she was closing the book, she saw a corner of a small piece of paper sticking out of the edge of the cover. She carefully removed it. It was a very old faded sepia photo of a family. There was a couple that looked like the parents, a young girl holding a baby, and two older boys. They were dressed like peasants. They weren't smiling. In the background it looked like a field of some sort. There was nothing written on it or on the back. Sophie stared at the photo for a long time. This has to be a clue of some kind. Where can I go to get more information about this? She gave up pondering about the photo and searched through the box for anything else. She picked up the birth certificates again and compared the two more closely. They seemed the same at first, but the difference was so slight as if they were not made at the same time or from the same source. She put it aside and decided to quit for the day. *I'll look at this in the morning. Maybe I will see things differently then.*

A few weeks later, after visiting her mother every day and watching her decline, Sophie decided to return to work. The doctor told her that her mother was being well taken care of, and she would not know if Sophie visited or not. Besides, her mother did not recognize Sophie anymore. As Sophie was packing and arranging for a flight back to New York, the dreaded phone call came. Her mother had passed away in her sleep and Sophie needed to make final arrangements.

It was a cold drizzly February as Sophie and Tessa walked through Metairie Cemetery where her mother was being buried. They were the only ones there as Sophie had no other family and what few friends her mother had were either too old and sick or were already gone. Sophie looked around the cemetery at all the sizes and shapes of the above ground graves and remarked, "What a beautiful and sad photograph this would make, the city of the dead."

Tessa gave her an odd look.

"I guess that was a heartless remark. Thinking about photographs at my mother's grave."

"It was a bit strange, but that is who you are, a photographer at heart. Maybe it would be a good memory to keep a photograph of where you parents are buried."

"This is where it will end for all of us. Then what? We're gone and forgotten. Will we become a footnote in someone's memory? Who will remember us when we are gone? You have children, Tessa, but I have no one. Maybe I should have married Wayne and had that nice life we planned."

"As you know, it wasn't such a nice life for me. My plan didn't exactly work out either.."

"Maybe I'm having a mid life crisis." Sophie laughed at her musings. "I don't know where to go or what to do next."

"This is not a time to plan anything. You go back home, you go to work, and after a time, something will come to you and you will be on the next part of your journey."

"We have become quite the philosophers." Sophie said as they left.

Sophie resumed looking through her parents papers when she was struck with another bombshell. In her mother's bank account there was a sizable amount, thousands of dollars. She thought maybe it was from a life insurance policy from her father, but as she examined the bank statements, she found monthly deposits of a couple of thousand dollars. These deposits went back for years. The oldest statement was dated from when Sophie was a little girl. She never knew her parents had that much money. She decided to go to the bank to get more information. The manager there told her it was not from any insurance company or retirement fund, but from a law firm in Chicago, and they could not give her any more information until she produced the proper paperwork that gave her the right to the information. She needed birth and death certificates for herself and her parents, which would take a while to obtain.

While waiting for the paperwork, she decided to return to New York to work only to find that her emotions were still in conflict. She discussed her feelings with her boss, Martin who had become a friend over the years.

"Do you want more time off? Are there more things you need to do back home?"

"No. I think I just need to get back into the

routine. Losing both my parents has made me feel sort of empty. When I get back to business, maybe this feeling will go away."

Sophie was involved in a new project when she obtained the death certificates for both her parents. When she returned to New Orleans she brought the documents to the bank. She was able to close out the account and given the information about the Chicago law firm that had sent the deposits. She called the firm directly but they could not or would not give her any information. She decided to go there in person.

CHAPTER SEVEN

Chicago. Sophie remembered that her parents came here every other year when she was young. It was the year that they came here without Sophie after she had just finished college when Sophie and Tessa found the documents in the attic about Phillip. Sophie looked around at the building she was about to enter where the law firm was. It didn't seem familiar but the museum was just around the corner where her mother used to take her when her father took care of business.

At first she was told that there was no information about the account she was inquiring about. Sophie went higher up in the company and was still told they had no information. Feeling as if she was being given the run around, and not understanding why, she decided she would go directly to the CEO. She was told that the CEO was unavailable, and would not even give her his name. They wouldn't even tell her where his office was. Since security was extremely tight, she planned to find out who he was and where he lived and go to his home. Although this seemed to be an extreme measure, this was the only clue she had about her parents mysterious secrets, so she felt that she had to pursue it, no matter what the outcome. She went to the library to find out who the CEO was. She found his name in one of the business directories and was then able to look up his address. She took a cab to that address, but was unable to get into the gated community's security. She returned to her hotel to figure out her next move.

She knew what he looked like because his picture was in the directory at the library, so she decided to wait in the lobby of the bank until she saw him. When she saw him arrive from the parking garage, he went straight to the elevators. She hurried to catch the same one he entered. He pressed the 15th floor. Sophie then confronted him. "Hello. You must be Mr. Novak, Hugh Novak"

"Yes. And who are you?"

Sophie knew she only had a minute before they came to the 15th floor. Being in the elevator, she knew he would be a captive audience, so she had to say what she planned to say quickly. "Mr. Novak, I'm Sophie St. Pierre. I have been trying to find out from your bank why you were sending my parents a great deal of money over the past years. I have seen three people, supervisors who can't seem to find out anything. That's a lot of money that your bank can't seem to trace. My parents are gone now, so that money is mine but I need to know where it came from. I'm asking you to please trace it for me. I find it hard to believe that so much money can be sent to my parents and no one here seems to know anything about it."

Hugh Novak looked at Sophie with an unreadable expression. Was it disinterest? Scorn? Boredom? Dismissal? Sophie could not tell. When the elevator opened, Mr. Novak exited the elevator, then turned to Sophie and said, "Follow me."

He led her to his office and told her to sit down. "Give me the information that you have and I will look it up."

"Thank you so much, Mr. Novak. I'm sorry to have confronted you this way, but no one would help or let me in to see you, and I'm trying to find answers to many secrets that my parents had."

After a few minutes of research on his computer, Mr. Novak said, "There doesn't seem to be any information on here about that account. You said that transfers have been going on for a number of years? Do you know when it started?"

"According to my parents bank, the deposits have been going on since I was a child. They never told me about any of that, and I know they didn't have any relatives that I know about. It is very strange and one of a couple of secrets they kept from me. If I am to keep this money, I need to know who it is from and why it was sent to my parents. Can't you find out anything on your computer?"

"Of course, you can find information on computers, but only what has been entered into it. We only have information from the last few years since banks started using computers. If this account was set up many years ago, the information has not been transferred to it. We have people working on going backwards entering previous accounts, but they haven't gone back that far yet. It will take some time to research this in the many boxes in the basement from old accounts." He said.

"How long do you think it would take?" asked Sophie.

"Miss St. Pierre, there are thousands of boxes down there. I can't give you a time. I would have to assign someone to look up your account. I'm not sure we can afford to pay someone just for you." he said rather testily.

"There is a considerable amount of money my parents left me. I'll write you a check to pay your employee to find my information. This is very important to me, Mr. Novak. There are secrets that my parents kept from me and this is the only clue I have. I need answers to those secrets."

"Very well. I'll see what I can do. As I said, this will take some time. Give my your address and phone number and I will contact you when I have something to tell you."

Sophie gave him her New York and New Orleans addresses and phone numbers, and her work number. "Thank you sir. I'll expect to hear from you soon."

Hugh Novak picked up the phone as soon as Sophie left his office.

Sophie returned to New York and tried to concentrate on her work. It was only a week later that she got the expected call, but it would be unlike anything that she could have ever imagined.

"Hello?" Sophie answered the phone.

"Hello Ms. St Pierre?"

"This is she. Who's calling?"

"My name is Cedric. I'm an attorney. Mr. Novak got in touch with me and told me of your situation. I have some news for you."

"You do? I'm listening. Did you find out who was putting money into my parents account for years?" asked Sophie.

"It's more than that. I'd like you to come to my office so we can discuss this."

"What do you mean? What more information do you have?"

"Please, Ms. St. Pierre. You need to come to

the office. It is too complicated to discuss over the phone. Beside I have some documents to give you."

"Documents? That sounds curious. What kind of documents do you have?"

"I can only tell you that I have been in contact with your parents over the years, and they wanted me to get in touch with you when the time was right."

"I don't understand."

"I know. It's complicated. I am available tomorrow if you can come to my office. I am in New York not far from where you are." He gave her the address.

"Yes, of course. I can be there at 8."

Sophie didn't sleep well wondering what Cedric had to tell her, and what kind of documents he had. Maybe she would finally get some answers about who Phillip was and where all those deposits to their bank came from.

Sophie looked down on Central Park from the 24th floor of Cedric's corner office. The floor to ceiling window gave an extraordinary view of New York. On the wall was the famous photograph of hers that she won an award for. There was something familiar about him and his office. "I've been here before, haven't I? I remember looking out of this window when I was a little girl. My parents used to come here to see you." She looked at his silver grey hair and the scar that went through the left side of his ear where part of his ear was missing. "I remember looking at that scar and being afraid of you."

"Yes, every other year they would come here. You would sit on the floor by the window and stare at me and the view. The last time you were here, you were ten. After that, your father would come alone to see me while your mother took you sightseeing."

"Why did they do that?" asked Sophie.

"You were old enough to become curious, so your parents told you it was just business. Please sit down. We have a lot to discuss. Can I get you some coffee?"

"Yes, thank you."

"First of all I have a letter from your parents. It will answer a lot of questions that you have. I suggest that you take some time to read it before we continue. You can have some privacy in the room next door. I'll see to it that you are not disturbed."

As much as Sophie wanted answers, she had a sinking feeling about reading the letter. She was anxious to find out the secret that her parents had kept from her, but she was nervous and afraid to find out. She opened the letter with dread and began to read.

Dearest Sophie,

Please understand that we loved you very much. What we did or did not tell you was not our choice, but was part of the arrangement we made with the parities involved. We wanted so much to explain it to you, but because we loved you so much we didn't want to hurt you. By the time you were old enough to understand, you were so involved with your career and enjoying your life so much, that we didn't want to put a damper on your excitement.

You may have found out or suspected by now that you were adopted. That does not change the way we felt about you as we always loved you just the same as if you were our biological child. We tried for years to have children, but there was one misfortune after another. I had already had two miscarriages, but one baby I carried almost to term. He was premature and died shortly after birth. We named him Philip. He was born and died on Christmas Eve.

A chill ran up Sophie spine as she continued reading.

A distant cousin of mine kept in touch with me through the years. He knew of the hardships I had trying to have a child. He was an American pilot in WWII. He was flying over France on a mission when he was shot down by the Germans. A group of Resistance fighters rescued him and his cousin who was also in the plane. They spent the next couple of months with the French Resistance until they could be picked up and returned to London. During the time he spent in France, he fell in love with one of the women of the Resistance. It was a very dangerous time then and no one knew if the next day would be their last. He and the French woman had a brief but serious affair. They are your biological parents.

After returning to London, your father continued flying missions until the war was over. He was wounded near the end of the war and spend time in the hospital recovering. When he finally was discharged and went home, his family gave him his belongings, which they kept from him while he was recuperating. There were a couple of letters from the French woman who told him that she was pregnant. They were unable to keep in touch during the war so he was unaware of the baby before.

When he was recovered enough to travel, he returned to France to find her and the child. It had been over three years since they parted. He went to the place where he was shot down to see if she was there, but there was no one left there who could tell him what happened to her. Eventually he found one of the Resistance members who told him that the woman was killed in a bombing. Sadly, he was going to return home, but decided to visit the place where she was killed. There he found that there was a baby who was rescued from the bombing. Circumstances surrounding the event of that day determined that the baby was his. The family that rescued the child came to love her as if she were their own. They had no way of knowing who she was and because everyone was involved in rebuilding after the war, no one had the time to find any information about her. After your father found you, he spent some time getting the paperwork in order to bring you to America. The French family who took care of you were devastated to lose you.

While he was in France working to bring you home, he got in touch with us to make arrangements for us to adopt you. He felt he was unable to take care of you since he was alone and wounded. Because of the morals of the times, he felt he could not tell his parents about you. They were a strict religious family and would not have approved of a child born of an affair.

We were overjoyed to become your parents. You were a godsend. We could not have loved you more if you were born to us.

Please don't think badly of us for not telling you this before, we wanted to tell you so many times, but the conditions of the adoption prevented us from doing so. We had asked him many times as you grew older to let us tell you the truth and have you know him as your father, but he always refused. As time went on, as he became involved with a new family and his business, it became harder for him to want the truth to come out. He did see you at the attorney's office each time we went there, and was kept advised of your life. He attended your graduations and other events where he could see you from afar and remain anonymous in a crowd. He did love you very much.

You should also realize that we were a couple with moderate means. While your father worked hard at his job, I wanted to stay home to be with you and give you all the love and attentions that I could. Your biological father made sure that we had the finances for me to stay home and send you to the best schools and to see that you were never without. We could never have afforded to send you to Tulane without his help. We never asked him for money, he gave it willingly and lovingly for your support.

Cedric has a letter that he wrote to you. Take your time reading it. Your father can explain much better than we can about himself and your mother. Their story is sad and wonderful at the same time.

Please listen to Cedric and consider all of his advise before you make any decisions about what he has to offer you. He has been involved in this since the beginning and is aware of everyone's feelings. We know that you will choose what is best for you. We have always been very proud of everything that you have done and chosen for your life.

Do not let this information disturb you or change your plans for the future. We trust you will continue to be the wonderful person that we raised you to be. We hope that your life will continue to be that wonderful event that you have been experiencing since your graduation.

With all our love,
Mom and Dad.

Sophie read and re-read the letter trying to absorb it all. Yes she did suspect that her parents had some secret and she even wondered if she might have been adopted, but this letter was proof. It gave her some answers, but not all. She stared out the window for a long time watching the people below going about their normal business while she was suffering this enormous shock. When there was a knock on the door, Sophie realized that she had tears on her cheeks and was wiping them off as Cedric entered the room and asked her if she was ok.

"I'm fine. It is a lot to think about. I suspected that there was something that my parents were not telling me, and even thought I might have been adopted, but many children want to think that so I dismissed it as a childhood fantasy."

"Do you want to go home to think about this more to get used to the idea, or do you want to continue?" Cedric asked.

"I'd like to continue now. I assume that there is a lot more you have to tell me, and I still have a lot of questions."

"Yes, quite a bit more. Shall we go back into my office?"

"In the letter my parents said that my father would see me in your office when we came here. I remember a man with a cane that was always here when we were. Was that him?"

"Yes that was him. And that brings me to the next letter. I have here a letter that he wrote to you.

It's a rather long one. You can go back to the other room to read it if you want. It might take you all evening to read it. Or, if you prefer, you can take it home and take as much time as you need to read it. When you are done, you can call me and we can discuss the rest."

"What else can you tell me? What else is there to know?"

"He wanted you to know about himself and your biological mother. He wrote to you about them and their history."

"What were their names?"

"Your father's name was Walter and you mother's Yvette. You should read his letter and let him tell you about them. But if you would rather skip that, we can continue this discussion. It's rather late though. You should go home and think about it. You may want to spend some time anyway to absorb this news."

"Yes. I think I'd like to go home. I really need some time to get used to the idea that my life was not what I thought it was."

"You are wrong there, Sophie. You had a good life, and are still having a good life, no matter who your parents were. They all loved you, and that's all that really matters."

"Yes, of course. You're right. I'll take this letter home and read it when I'm ready. I'll call you soon. Thank you, Cedric."

Sophie could not read the letter right away. She thought she should return to work to have something to do to clear her mind. But she couldn't concentrate. She knew she wanted more answers, but was afraid of what she might learn. Up until now, her life seemed to have gone in a direction of her choosing, but with the unanswered questions about her parent's secret, she wondered what else they hid from her. Who were her real parents? She was ready to find out. She began reading the letter that Cedric said was from her biological father.

Dear Sophie,

Since you are reading this, you have already seen Cedric and know that I am you father. I'm sorry to have kept it a secret from you, and am sorry that I insisted that your adoptive parents not tell you. It was a condition that I made with them many years ago when they adopted you, and once made became hard to break. I agreed that they could tell you at the right time, but I never knew what the right time was, and kept putting it off. Please do not blame them for not telling you. They did a wonderful job of raising you, I could not have chosen better people to do so. Your mother was a cousin of mine who wanted children, but was unable to successfully carry a child. She had a baby boy who was premature and did not live a day. Because of these misfortunes, she was very unhappy. When I found you, I felt that I was unable to take care of a child at that time. Your biological mother was killed in the war and had no family that I could find. I turned to my cousin to have them adopt you. I believe that I made the right decision then and I still do. You have become a successful and talented person and we are all proud of you.

I would like to tell you about your mother and I. This is the story about us and how we met.

I was born in London shortly after World War

I. My father and his brothers were in the printing business. They had visited America before the war and wanted to expand their business by opening an office in the United States. My father and one of his brothers emigrated their families to America when I was ten. They set up a printing business in New Jersey called *Walter and Theodore Printing Company,* the same name as in London. They eventually became American citizens.

My uncle also had a son, Theo, who was the same age as myself. We did everything together. As teenagers we were wild and adventuresome. We became interested in airplanes and took flying lessons. We had so much fun that we wanted to become pilots. After we got our license, we flew everywhere. We were reckless and did some dangerous things, but we were having the time of our lives.

Then in 1940, World War ll started. The Germans invaded France and began bombing Britain. My parents were horrified as we had family there and they were worried about them. America had not joined the military action yet, but was part of the Allied pact. Theo and I wanted to join the Air Force, but America was not sending pilots yet. We wanted to be part of the fighting, not because of a loyalty to family and country, but because we were young and looking for that great adventure. When Japan bombed Pearl Harbor and America joined the war, we were anxious to be part of the action but we were turned down by the military as we did not meet the qualifications of the United States Air Force.

Our families in London were sending us the messages about the radio broadcasts by Charles de Gaulle and the Free French. We learned of the many groups of Resistance fighters all over France and how pilots from the Allies were supplying the resistance with guns, ammunition, radios, equipment, and spies. We heard about someone in London recruiting pilots, and about the Royal Canadian Air Force accepting pilots that were turned down by the Americans. Because they badly needed pilots, we were accepted into the Eagle Squadron. We went through a quick training to fly Supermarine Spitfires and flew bombing raids of German bases in France. We also flew men and supplied into the occupied part of Northern France. We were still reckless and daring but flew many successful missions.

We also learned to fly Lysanders, another type of plane, with specifications for different types of missions. The Lysanders were larger planes that dropped supplies to Resistance fighters. They were able to land in small fields for pick-ups and deliveries. We were assigned one when the regular pilot was too sick to fly. We were flying over Northern France in a clandestine mission to a predestined location to drop supplies to the Resistance there, but we were shot down by the Germans. We were able to eject before the plane crashed. Theo and I were found miles apart by the Resistance. We sustained minor injuries. The Resistance had to hide us from the Germans since our plane was shot down, because they might be looking for survivors. But when the Germans found out that the plane blew up after the crash, they stopped looking for us. The Resistance were able to send a message to London that we survived and received a message back that we could be rescued soon. Many of the missions in the Lysanders that would land to pick up people would only fly during the full moon, so we would have to wait for the next one. During the wait we helped the Resistance fighters however we could. They were camped out mostly in the woods to hide from the Germans, and got help and supplies from nearby farms and vineyards. We ended up staying a couple of months because each month when the moon full there were problems, such as bad weather, that prevented our rescue.

The months that we spent there changed us. We got to know the Resistance fighters and were humbled by them. We saw and experienced horrors and heroes. We learned that ordinary people will take extraordinary measures to fight for what they believe in. We saw how the people who witnessed the horrendous acts by the German soldiers against innocent people, stepped in and risked their lives to right that wrong. We learned what it meant to be human.

One of the Resistance fighters was a beautiful young French woman. Her name was Yvette. Her love for her country was an inspiration. She was incredibly brave. While we were stranded, we helped out as much as we could, going out on missions around the area, delivering supplies and picking up messages to transmit back to London. I accompanied her on most of these missions. It was sometimes frightening, always exciting, and our emotions were high. In a time like that during the war when you don't know if the next day could be your last, we felt that we had to live fully and completely every day. Falling in love like that, thinking that there might not be a tomorrow, was like an explosion of emotions. It was an awful and wonderful time for lovers. We knew that every minute of every day counted and we made the most of it. I have never felt so alive as I did then.

I have never loved like that again.

Theo also fell in love with one of the women. Her name was Hélène. We wanted to stay with them and continue helping them, but with a war going on, we were needed elsewhere. We vowed to return when the war was over.

Then we were rescued and I had to leave her. There was a war to be won and I couldn't take her with me or stay with her. Before I got on the rescue plane, I gave her my address in the States. We couldn't stay in touch with each other because even if we had written letters, Germans would have censored them. Many letters were torn up and thrown away. We could not get messages through the radio because they were used for more important communications.

Theo and I were sent on many other missions. In one of them we were again shot down, but this time we were wounded and captured by the Germans and were sent to a concentration camp. By this time the war was officially over. It was 1944 and the Americans had landed on Normandy Beach. That was just the beginning of the end of the war. We spent a few months in the concentration camp before we were rescued because it took the Allies some time to find all of the camps and evacuate all of the prisoners. We did not get decent medical treatment while we were in the concentration camp. Due to our injuries, we were transported to a hospital in London. By that time my wounds were so severe that I had to have my leg amputated. I spent months in the London hospital before I was sent home to a hospital in America where I went through more surgeries and rehabilitation. It wasn't until I was finally discharged and sent home that I received the letters from your mother. My family had kept some of my things in a box not thinking that I wanted to see any of it. So it was a couple of years after we last saw each other before I finally knew what had happened to her. That's when I found out that she was pregnant. By then it had been over three years since we had been in France. Theo and I wanted to return to France to find the women, but when we found out that they each had a child, we were anxious to see them again and take them home with us to America.

Even after the war, communication was difficult. Our only hope to find them was to go back to France.

We were able to find the location where we were shot down. From there, we made our way to the vineyard where we had hidden out. It was abandoned. No one was there. The neighbors did not know what happened to the family that lived there. They remembered that the owner, Henri, had two children but when the war was over, none of them returned. We went to the nearby town questioning many people until we finally found someone that we remembered who was in the Resistance group. All they knew was that the women, Yvette and Hélène both had a child. Even though they were pregnant, they continued to work with the Resistance. They used their pregnancy to hide documents under their clothes. After their babies were born, they took them on other missions hiding documents in their babies' carriages and clothes. They were last seen taking a train to Amiens where they heard that there was a mission to rescue important Resistance members who were in a prison there. After that, the women never returned home.

We went to Amiens to find that the train never

arrived there. The train was bombed before it reached its destination, but the mission was partly successful as many Resistance members were able to escape. When the women did not return from the mission it was assumed that they were killed.

We were devastated by the news that the women were killed and would have returned home. Someone convinced us to visit the town to find out what happened there.

In the town near Amiens where the train was bombed, we found the villagers who agreed to talk to us about the disaster and that there were survivors. They led us to the Ducros family. They were reluctant to talk to us at first, but eventually told us about the baby that they rescued from the wreck. The only other survivors were German soldiers. The women did not survive. We were shocked and saddened by the news. All we wanted was to return to France and find Yvette and Hélène and take them to America with us.

The villagers figured out that the baby had to belong to one of the women because there were no other women on that train. But they could not find out who the baby belonged to, so they raised her as their own. They told us that they thought the women and babies might have been German, but there was no way to find out. Their daughter, Dominique who was thirteen when we arrived helped raise the baby and became very attached to her. Since the family spent a lot of time repairing the vineyards from the devastation brought on by the war, Dominique was given the responsibility to care for the baby. She was devastated when we took the baby away.

It took some time to get the paperwork in order, but we finally were able to bring the baby to

America. I was young and severely wounded and felt unable to take care of a child. I had a cousin in New Orleans whom I kept in touch with. I knew that she had been trying to have children, but had not been able to carry a child to term. Her last pregnancy had resulted in a premature baby who did not live long. The boy, Philip, died on Christmas Eve.

I felt that she and her husband would be good parents. When I discussed the possibility of them adopting you, they readily agreed. I had no birth certificate for you, but knew that you were born sometime in December, close to the time that your parents had lost their little boy, so we chose that date for your birth certificate. My parents were in the printing business so it was easy to make up a certificate that looked genuine.

I wanted you to have the very best of everything. Your parents were not well off, so I made sure that they had the funds to give you everything you needed. All of the arrangements were made through the attorney that you met, Cedric. We met Cedric in London at the base where we were stationed. His father was a lawyer and after the war, Cedric went to school on the G.I. Bill and became a lawyer himself. Since then he has handled everything. I trust him with my life. I hope you will trust him too and listen to his advise.

I have followed your life and am very proud of what you have become. Your parents sent me photographs and reports and kept me up to date of everything you did. Every time they came to New York to meet with Cedric, that gave me a chance to see you in person, although no one was to tell you who I was. When you became old enough to question the reason for the visits, your parents stopped taking you to the office, and your mother would take you sightseeing.

I attended your high school and college graduations, and a few other events where there was a crowd that I could remain anonymous in. I was very involved in your life. There were many times that I wanted to tell you the truth. Your parents and I discussed when would be the best time to tell you, but we always found an excuse to put it off. At first it was because of my injuries, and the way my life was going, then it was that your life was going so well that we didn't want to upset you. Maybe it would not have upset you, maybe it would not have made a difference, but it was our way of coping and we thought at the time it was the best way to handle things. There were times when we thought that you would never need to know, and other times when we thought it was inevitable that you would find out. We never meant to hurt you by not telling you. You are a remarkable person and I hope you don't blame any of us for our decisions. Everything we did was out of love for you. We have been and always will be proud of you.

Your mother was a remarkable person too. I loved her very much. It is time for you to get to know her. This is her story.

PART THREE

CHAPTER EIGHT

"*Papa! C'est moi.*" Yvette called to her father. Where are you? I'm home."

"What are you doing here? I thought you were in school." Henri Legier answered.

"The University is moving. The Germans have invaded the Alsace-Lorraine area, and our teachers are worried."

"The University of Strasbourg is moving? How can they do that?"

"The professors think the Germans will take over the school and tell them what they can and cannot teach. My friends watched in horror as the Germans barged in and some of the professors were taken in for questioning. No one knows what to do. The administration is moving the University to Clermont-Ferrand outside of the occupied zone. They feel that they will still be able to teach freely there. The professors told us to return home to wait. Many students and teachers left as soon as the Germans arrived. Everyone is afraid."

"Why were they questioning some of the teachers? Were they doing something wrong?"

"We don't know. There was some talk about groups of people doing things to sabotage the Germans. Maybe the Germans thought that the teachers knew something about those rumors, but I thought they were only rumors."

"Tell me about those rumors. I have heard some too. What do the Germans think is going on?" her father asked.

"Some of my friends said that there are groups of people all over the country, here in the occupied area as well as in the South who are doing clandestine things to the Germans. Many people are angry about the occupation and think we should all be doing something about it. There are groups of people forging documents because we have to use coupons for food, but for many, the coupons are not enough to survive on. The Germans are taking our food and other things and sending it all to Germany."

"What about you? What do you think?"

"At first, the Germans acted like they were our friends and came here to help us, but they are arrogant and have a cruel side to them. I don't like the Germans. They are a very scary people. They think they can come here and take over our country. I'm afraid for us."

"What else can you tell me? Do you know anyone personally who is in these groups? That's a very dangerous place to be."

"I only know what my friends say. I heard that someone cut a telephone line in a town where the Germans were setting up. The Germans were so angry that when they found out who did it, they shot him. They set it up as an example so no one else would do anything against them."

"Did you have any problems getting home?"

"Hélène, Cécile and I and some other students took the train back. There were German soldiers everywhere. We just wanted to come home. Where is my brother? I don't see him anywhere. Isn't he supposed to be working out in the fields?"

"Jean-Paul is out doing an errand. He'll be back later."

Yvette knew more than she admitted to her father. She knew the boy who cut the telephone line and what happened to him. The teachers told the students to go home because they suspected that the Germans knew what some of the teachers were doing and thought they might be arrested. They didn't want to put the students in danger while the school was being moved to Clermont-Ferrand. And then there were a few teachers suspected of working with the Germans. Why they would do that, she did not know. Her friends suspected that the informers were trying to get in good graces with the Germans because they thought the Germans were eventually going to win and take over all of France. Many people accepted this even though they deplored the idea, they didn't know how to fight them when the military had failed so miserably. But a few brave people vowed to do something about it. They were not going to submit peacefully to the German occupation. They started doing little things like forging documents and cutting telephone lines. Yvette and her friends were involved in copying food and fuel coupons, giving them out to the people who were hungry. Some of the teachers were responsible for starting the groups. They were careful in selecting students to help, finding out their priorities during class. They carefully suggested things for the students to do until they thought they could trust them. Then the responsibilities grew from there. Yvette was afraid to tell her father, although she knew he hated the Germans, she heard of some families who reported their own people for favors from the Germans. She didn't think her father would ever do such a thing, but in these strange times, Yvette thought it best not to tell her father. She also didn't want to upset him, knowing he would be worried about her.

Henri was not going to tell his daughter about what he and Jean-Paul had been doing. He did not want to upset his daughter and have her worry about them, not knowing that she was also doing undercover activities. Henri knew that Jean-Paul was out helping to derail a train that was carrying German soldiers and supplies.

As the German occupation continued, what bothered the French people the most was the shortage of supplies, and the fact that the Germans were not only taking over their country, but taking over their livelihood by confiscating most of what they had and sending it to Germany. They took their food, supplies, and even artwork and sent it all to Germany. They even recruited able bodied young men and sent them to the German factories, some of which were making guns and ammunition in which to fight the French with.

Jean-Paul barged in out of breath. Not seeing his sister, he blurted out, "It is done, Papa. The train will not get to its destination." Then he stopped short when he saw Yvette. "What are you doing here? I thought you were in school."

"What did you do? Why are you so excited and out of breath?"

"Come and give me a hug first. I haven't seen you in a while. How are your studies going?" As he hugged his sister, he looked over her shoulder at their father for some sign that she knew what they were up to, but Henri just shrugged his shoulders and shook his head no.

Henri interrupted them, "Let's eat first. You must both be starving. I was just finishing this soup with vegetables from the garden."

"You have vegetables Papa? I thought the Germans confiscated all we had planted."

"Yes, Yvette. I have plenty vegetables. The neighbors and I had too much for the Germans to take it all, but we are sure they will be back, so we found a remote location that the Germans won't find, and we take turns planting, cultivating and sharing, so none of us will go hungry."

After they ate, Yvette asked Jean-Paul to explain where he was when he barged in so out of breath, and Jean-Paul asked her again why she was not in school. Eventually they got into a discussion about the German occupation and Marshal Petain. Petain, being a hero from the first World War, was chosen to represent the French government, but it was becoming clear to many that he was collaborating with the Germans. "Petain just signed an armistice with Hitler not far from here in Compiègne. Hitler insisted on that place because it was where Germany had to sign the treaty ending the war that they had lost before. Hitler was making a fool of us." Henri said disgustedly.

"I think it is deplorable how many of our people accept this occupation. Can't they see how horrible the Germans are? Why don't they do something?" Yvette implored.

"Many people think it is inevitable that we will end up under Nazi rule because they are so powerful. Because Hitler, Stalin, and Mussolini have joined forces to overcome all of Europe, it seems inevitable that we will lose. Not only that, but Japan has also signed a Pact with them forming the Axis Powers. Half the world is joining Hitler. We will be attacked by Germany, Russia and Italy, from all sides, so we might as well accept it and cooperate so we are not punished, then we will not have to suffer anymore. Others don't like it but feel helpless about what they can do." Jean-Paul explained.

Henri added, "After the terrible war that I was in, so many of our people were killed and many more wounded, I can't believe we are living through this again. The Germans continue to take what they want. They have no respect for the French people, or anyone else in the world, for that matter. They have just bombed Britain, but thanks to the British and the Allies, the Germans were defeated. At least someone put up a fight and won against them."

"How do you know what is happening in Britain?" asked Yvette.

"I hear the truth about what is happening over the radio. First, Marshal Petain announced that they will be signing an armistice. He believes that we cannot win against the Germans and we must give in so they can take over. He seems to believe that we will not lose any more soldiers if we give in. I think he is getting too old to rule us. A few days later we heard from Charles de Gaulle and the Free French broadcasting news from London on the BBC. De Gaulle said that 'the flame of French resistance must not and shall not die.' I believe he might be the one who can help us fight the Germans."

"You are listening to him on the radio?" asked Yvette. "They will not allow us to listen to anything but Radio Nationale."

"Well they can't monitor every one of us every minute of every day." Jean-Paul replied.

"What else are you both doing? I know listening to the radio is not the only thing you would do against the Germans."

"You are right. My friends and I have been planning submissive activities against the Germans."

"You are doing more than planning. You just diverted a train. That is more dangerous than what I was doing. I am afraid for you."

"The Germans will never find out who we are. We are very careful to disappear after our attacks." Jean-Paul told Yvette about the other trains carrying German soldiers and supplies that they had derailed, and about how they cut communication lines the Germans set up.

Yvette told her brother and father how she and her friends were taught how to print false documents and coupons to deliver to those who needed them. She explained how some of her teachers carefully chose the students that they thought would help, but somehow there was someone who was an informer and a couple of teachers were arrested. The administration decided to shut down the school and move it to Clermont-Ferrand in the unoccupied zone. She planned to return to school when it reopened. "While I am not in school, I don't know how to help without the guidance of the professors. I want to do more. I need to do more. I can't sit by while so many need help. Let me help you. Give me something to do."

"What we are doing is too dangerous for you."

"I am already in danger if those teachers who were arrested reveal our names. Please let me help."

"I don't want Papa to worry about you too. Isn't that right Papa?"

"I agree, it is dangerous, but I have lived

through what the Germans did to us in the last war. If more people had done more then, we might not be in this position today. I can never forgive or forget that, because of that war you mother died. She was weakened by hunger while I was away fighting, and even after the war was over she never fully recovered. Giving birth to you both was hard on her, especially when she was pregnant with you, Yvette. She died shortly after you were born. I miss her every day and I'm sad that she died, but I love you both none the less for that. Someone has to act so that this doesn't happen again especially to our young people. Too many have died in the last war. We must stop the Nazis from destroying our country again. If you both believe strongly in our country, then you will do what you think is right. Do what you have to do and I will help you as much as I can. No matter what. I will be proud of you both.

Jean-Paul and his friend Raymond invited the girls to the camp where they would decide what to do and where to strike next. Suddenly two of their friends who were in school at the Sorbonne in Paris rushed into the meeting. Edmond was out of breath as he reported the incident, "The situation in Paris is getting worse. We were going to the celebrate Armistice Day at the Tomb of the Unknown Soldier. The Germans did not want us to celebrate since it was the war that they lost. We were told in school that the Germans forbade us to go, but we wanted to pay our respects, so we disobeyed the order. We were angry that they would tell us we can't honor our soldiers who died in the war. As we were making our way there, hundreds of others were also going. This gave us encouragement. As we marched from the

Place de l'É'toile to the Arc de Triomphe, there were thousands of us."

Louise who was with Edmond continued the story. "We started singing *La Marseillaise* and shouting *Vive la France*. There were German soldiers and SS everywhere. At first they ignored us but then they started grabbing and arresting people. Then shots rang out and everyone started running in every direction. I don't know if anyone was killed because we ran back to the school. But the soldiers were there too, so we ran to the train station and came home."

Edmond continued. "We were so afraid when they started shooting at us. How can they do that to us? We were only having a peaceful gathering to honor our soldiers. The Germans are becoming horrible to us. They want to take over our country and control everything we do. We can't let this continue. My friends, we have to start doing more to get them out of our country."

"*Mon Dieu*, this is terrible. This proves that there is no peaceful way to live under German rule. They would kill us all to take over our land." said Yvette.

Jean-Paul replied, "Yes we are going to have to do more than stopping trains and forging papers."

"Have you heard about the coal miner's strike?" Marc had just arrived to join the group and report on activities in the area. "The Germans took over the mines as well as the railway workers and textile industries for their own benefit and are paying the workers so little that they can't even support their families. My father and his friends and many others joined the strike. But the Germans have such control that they deported hundreds of the striking workers to a German prison camp. We can't even protest against them. If this keeps up, there will be no Frenchmen left alive."

"We cannot continue to live under German rule. We are less than animals to them. We must do more to stop them. We might have a chance. Hitler has invaded the Soviet Union. He has turned against Stalin. Now maybe Russia will join us in the fight to defeat Germany. We must recruit more people. We must tell London that we need guns and supplies." Raymond said.

They soon discovered that there was a network of people fighting for their freedom that was being established throughout France. People were realizing that the Germans were not going to stop the rape of France, no matter what they said in the Armistice. France was literally divided in half into two zones, where the occupied north was to be ruled by the Germans, and the south was to be free. But the Germans were still invading the south. The Vichy government was established in which Marshal Petain was supposed to be in charge, but it became clear that this government was collaborating with Germany, and Petain and the others were just puppets. At first the French people supported the Vichy government believing that if they cooperated, when Germany took over completely, they would be in their good graces. The Vichy government established a militia made up of Frenchmen looking for spies. Many Frenchmen turned against each other. But other Frenchmen, who listened to Charles de Gaulle over the radio from London began to form groups to fight the Germans however they could. London, along with the Allies, began supplying arms, ammunition, communication devices and people to help the groups, who were now being called the Resistance. The more the Germans tried to eradicate the Resistance groups by sending them to prison camps and even executing them on the spot, the more people joined with the Resistance. The Germans would capture and kill even innocent people, men, women, and children, who were reported to them by their spies. There was no trial, no jury. People would be taken away, shot, or just disappear.

The Resistance was becoming more organized. The worse the situation got, the more people were horrified and wanted to help the Resistance. They believed that the Allies would soon arrive to help them fight the Germans.

One hot summer night as the group was gathering what meager supplies they had, Raymond was strumming on his guitar. He knew some American tunes and was playing some Benny Goodman and Glenn Miller. The night was clear with a full moon. Raymond started playing *Blue Moon*, and they all joined in and sang with him. Edmond, who had gone back to Paris to see what was happening there, rushed back into the meeting. "I have bad news," he said. "I was waiting at a train station when someone shot a German soldier right out in the open in front of a crowd of people. I was with some friends that I was trying to recruit. One of my friends knew of this man named Pierre-Felix Geroges who we were about to talk to when Pierre shot the German. There were more shots but only the one soldier was killed. Pierre uses the name Fabien so that only the members of his group knew who he was."

Raymond replied, "That sounds like good news to me. One less German on this earth."

"But that is not the bad news! The Germans are so outraged that one of them was shot to death, that they executed a number of innocent French people in retaliation. They said that from now on, for every German soldier that is shot, they will kill a hundred Frenchmen."

"*Mon Dieu!* That is horrible. What can we do?" cried Yvette.

Everyone started shouting at once.

"Maybe we should kill more of them."

"Maybe we should stop what we are doing. It is getting more dangerous every day."

"Why aren't more people fighting them?"

"It is hopeless. We can't go on like this."

"We need to recruit more people."

"We need more guns and ammunition."

"Where are the Allies? Why are they taking so long to help us?"

Jean-Paul and Raymond let the people talk out their frustrations. Then they both stood up and shouted, "Stop! Listen! You all have opinions and most of them are good, but we need a plan. We have to become more organized. It is apparent that there are others throughout the country that believe as we do, and from what I hear, they are also doing the same things that we are doing. I hear of other train derailments and other subversive things going on everywhere, each doing their own thing. We need to contact them and see if we can get better organized. We need someone who can lead these groups, someone who can be in charge and get us help from our Allies. We need more supplies. We need more guns and ammunition. We need to become like an army. Then we might be able to do more damage to the Germans. But right now, we are all tired and upset. You should all get some sleep and then we can discuss this in the morning."

Yvette could see that her brother was becoming an effective leader. She noticed how the others respected him and listened to him. She thought he needed a little encouragement, so she took him aside and told him so. "You are doing a wonderful job. They look up to you for guidance. I think they will follow your lead and do whatever you ask of them."

"I hope you are right. I wonder what we are doing. Are we making a difference or making fools of ourselves."

"Remember what father said, we are doing what we believe in. We believe in our country and our future and for that we must keep on fighting. Even if we lose, at least we will not have given up. At least we can say we did our best. I'd rather die fighting than give up and live under German rule. And I think that they all believe that too."

"Yvette, you are the best sister anyone could have. I just hope..."

"Don't say it." Yvette hugged her brother tightly. "Get some sleep. We all need a rest. Everything will be clearer in the morning."

CHAPTER NINE

The little group of Resistance fighters continued recruiting more members. They continued their clandestine activities of derailing trains, cutting communication lines, forging documents giving some people new identities so they could travel unnoticed from the occupied zone to the free zone, and forging food, fuel and other coupons to give to those who needed them. While they were meeting in their forest hideout, Marc, who was traveling around the area to find out information on where the Germans were, hurried into the camp. "They've done it!" he exclaimed. "The Americans have finally officially entered the war.."

"Well it's about time. What happened to get them to help us?" Raymond asked.

"You haven't heard? The Japanese bombed Pearl Harbor. The Americans are outraged. President Roosevelt called it 'A day that will live in infamy.' He declared war on Japan. Then Germany and Italy declared war on the United States, so this has become a global war. It isn't just France and Britain and our European countries against Hitler anymore. It seems like the whole world is at war."

"So the powerful Americans got hit in their belly and they are now joining the rest of us to fight the enemy." Raymond said.

"Don't be so hard on the Americans." said Jean-Paul. "They have been helping. With that treaty with the British, they were giving them supplies that have helped us."

"Yes, but now that the are actively in this war, we will be getting more. Maybe we can win this. Maybe they will help us get the Germans out of our country." said Yvette.

While Jean-Paul, Raymond, Yvette, Hélène, and Cécile were continuing their activities, Marc and Edmond traveled around through the occupied and unoccupied zones finding out as much as they could about what the Germans were doing and where they were located. They also scouted out the Resistance groups for information that could help their own group. They learned that the Resistance were becoming more organized under leadership of people like Jean Moulin, Henri Frenay, Marie-Madeline Fourcade and others, and that the groups were able to keep in touch with London by means of the transmitters being sent to different areas. People and supplies were being dropped off at select locations throughout France. They brought this information back to the group to see what changes they could make.

"They want us to find locations for planes to drop supplies where the Germans are nowhere near. They also want to know if we can find a spot where a plane can land to pick up people. It needs to be a small level field, away from the town and well hidden." Marc reported.

"We know just the place." Jean-Paul said. "You remember that field eight miles from here? It is well hidden and there are no vineyards nearby so no one would hear a plane landing."

"The Germans have established a work force and are recruiting many young men to join. They call it *Service du Travail Obligatoire.* They said the men will be well paid and will return home later. They are being sent to German factories." said Edmond.

"How can any of our men join such a work force?" said Raymond."

"The Germans make it sound like it is voluntary, but it's not. They are rounding up all the young men they can find. You are not allowed to say no. It won't be long before they come here and find us."

"Many are refusing to go. That has been a big gain for the Resistance. These young men are joining the Resistance by the thousands, and many are starting up their own groups. But here is the problem. They cannot return home because the Gestapo will come for them. They are going into hiding in the forests and mountains. They are becoming like guerrillas, attacking the Germans wherever they can. They are called *Maquisards."*

"Then we will do the same. But we will not wait for the Germans to come here. We already have many good hiding places here in our forests." said Jean-Paul. "Go back and report to the Resistance leaders that we have an excellent location for their airplane drops."

Soon the Allies began using the fields near their vineyards to drop supplies and men. Jean-Paul's group of Resistance fighters were finding places to hide them. Some of their neighbors had evacuated to the south when the Germans first invaded and left their farms abandoned. Some farms had been abandoned after the first war when many men did not return, and their buildings, homes, vineyards and fields were left in disrepair. Jean-Paul and Raymond and their friends had played in the crumbling buildings when they were children, so they knew every nook and cranny in the old buildings and cellars where the group could hide supplies and soldiers who parachuted into the area.

One night a plane landed with a soldier who had radio transmitters among other things. He was brought to Henri's vineyard to hide out until it was safe for him to be brought to the Resistance headquarters nearby. Henri was fascinated with the transmitter and asked the soldier how it worked. He told the soldier that he would be willing to operate one for the Resistance since he was not able to go out on patrols with the younger people because of his old war injuries, and he wanted to do more than just hiding out people. When the soldier returned after delivering the transmitters, while waiting to be picked up by plane from London, he told Henri that the Gaullists in London accepted his idea and his location would be ideal for a transmitter. The soldier said he would return when he could with a transmitter and teach him how to use it.

A few months later the soldier did return. He spent the next few days teaching Henri how to receive and send messages and how to use the codes. Henri then found the perfect hiding place for it. In one of his old barns that was no longer in use, there was a stack of old wine barrels, many of them toppled over. Henri made a crawl space through a barrel at the bottom of the stack cutting out the bottom of the barrel in such a way that he could use it as a door. He could replace the cut out piece so it would not look like a door, and being at floor level, anyone searching would not think there was a crawl space inside the barrel. Even if they did look there, he replaced the back of the barrel and swept the dust around to look dirty and unused again. After crawling through the barrel, Henri set up the transmitter in another barrel that he cut out to make a desk of sorts. He cut out a side piece of a barrel and made a cabinet with a hinged door. He could open and close the door so that it looked like a normal old barrel when the door was closed. Then he rigged up an antenna under the mud floor and out the back of the barn, and up into the tree that was adjacent to the barn. The whole set-up was so camouflaged that Jean-Paul, Yvette and the others could not locate the hiding place. They felt sure that if the Germans barged in without notice, as they usually did, they would never find the transmitter.

After Henri was set up and began sending and receiving messages, he needed someone to deliver the messages to the Resistance leader groups at predestined locations. Yvette, Hélène and Cécile became the runners. A system was set up using the bookstore in the village. The girls would ride their bicycles to the village as if they were going shopping. They would wander around town window shopping or go to the market and buy something. Then the girls would go to the bookstore pretending to look for a book. A certain book was chosen that no one would be interested in buying, where someone had placed a message in between particular page numbers. The girls would retrieve the message and place another one for pick up. So that it would not look suspicious, they would not always go together. Sometimes it would be one, or two or all three girls would go to the bookstore, wander around as if looking for something interesting, even read for a while, and eventually locate the right book to exchange the messages. If anyone found the book and the message inside, they would not know what it was because all the messages were written in code. Even Henri did not know what the message said. The girls would hide the message in the bottom of a picnic basket, or the hem of their dress, or some other place where no one would look. Since they were pretty and young, the Germans did not suspect them. The girls would even smile or wave to the soldiers. The girls felt that they were finally doing something more important than forging documents, even though that was still important as food and supply coupons were severely rationed, and some of the Resistance members needed fake identification papers to travel around France gathering information.

Besides the coded messages, the Resistance were told that they must all have specific code names especially for when they were meeting members outside of their area. This was to protect their identity and the identity of their families. Many Resistance members were caught and tortured and some broke under the pressure and revealed the names of other members. By using the code names, the Germans would not know who the real person was, nor would the other Resistance members. Henri was given the code WASP for his transmissions. He was to begin his messages with WSP303.

Jean-Paul's group got together one evening to choose code names for themselves. "The large group that we get information from all chose animal names." said Raymond. "Their leader is Hedgehog and Eagle. I have met with others to exchange information and was told that it is becoming more important to use code names as so many members are being captured and tortured so badly that they give the Germans information. The Germans are becoming more vicious everyday. They call the group with the animal names, *'Noah's Ark,'* and are desperate to catch them all. I don't know any of their real identities and they don't want to know ours."

"They have all chosen animal names, so why don't we choose something different." said Marc.

"We would like to be flowers." said Cécile. "I think the men ought to be birds."

Their code names were chosen and from then on, they were to address each other with their *Noms de Guerre.*

Yvette was now Camellia, Hélène became Jasmine, and Cécile chose Lilac.

Jean-Paul's name was Hawk, and Raymond chose Raven.

CHAPTER TEN

One afternoon Henri received a message that there would be a Lysander plane landing in the field they had chosen. There had been a number of landings there and it was deemed to be a safe place. The landing would be at the full moon as all of the landings were. The group went to the designated area and waited. There was a signal they used to alert the plane. The Resistance members were to form a V and would light their lanterns when they heard the motor of the plane above, so the pilot would know where to land. But something went wrong this time. The Germans must have found out the location of the landing field. As the plane approached, the Resistance members heard the sound of heavy artillery. They gasped in horror as they saw the plane catch fire. They quickly put out their lanterns. Jean-Paul watched the sky carefully and said, "I think I see a parachute. Look. See if you can track where it is going to fall."

As the group was trying to follow the silhouette of the parachute against the darkened sky, they heard the sound of the plane crashing nearby. Then the sky lit up with the burning of the wreckage. It was then that they were able to see clearly where the parachute was going. Jean-Paul assigned some of the members to follow the parachute, and others to go to the wreckage. It took most of the night locating where the parachute landed. Before they found the soldier, they came across other items from the plane. When they found the soldier, he was trying to pull his parachute from the tree. He turned around sharply when he heard someone nearby, and pulled out his pistol.

"*Ne tirez pas. Nous sommes amis!*" shouted Jean-Paul with his hands up in surrender. "We are friend. We help."

The soldier cautiously looked around when Yvette said, "Friend, we are friend. German shot you down. We help you. Come quick. German near."

The soldier relaxed a bit, put his gun away, and started to fold up the parachute. "We have to get all of this out of here. We can't leave any trace that I parachuted out. Did you find my friend? I think he got out of the plane. And the supplies? Did you find any of the other stuff I dumped when I knew we were shot?"

Jean-Paul and Yvette looked at each other and at the soldier and shrugged their shoulders. "Come quick! We go. Germans near." They motioned the soldier to follow them.

They hid the soldier in the cellar one of Henri's empty barns along with what supplies they were able to recover. Yvette brought him a blanket and some food. "You sleep here. Germans patrolling near."

"Did you find my friend? Did you pick up any more of the supplies we dropped?" he asked.

Yvette shrugged her shoulders, "Sleep now. We look tomorrow." Then she left covering the cellar trap door with dust and rubble so that it was well hidden.

Henri and Yvette were back at the house getting ready for bed when the Germans barged in. "Where is soldier?"

"No soldier here." said Henri.

"Plane crashed, soldier escaped. We saw parachute." the Germans said.

"No soldier here." Henri repeated.

"We search property."

"Go search." Henri tried to be nonchalant. "I'm going to bed."

Since it was late and dark, the Germans did a cursory search. Henri and Yvette knew they would be back in the morning for a better search. They were glad that Jean-Paul went back to the forest hideout where he spent most of the time now.

In the morning, Yvette brought the soldier something to eat. He was sound asleep. She watched how peaceful he looked for sometime before she decided to awaken him.

"American. Wake. Eat." Yvette said in what English she knew.

"Thank you. *Merci.* Have you found my friend? And the packages?" He asked as he ate.

"You stay. Hide. Germans come back soon, search. Stay quiet. I return soon." Yvette left him, hoping he understood.

The German soldiers came back and searched more thoroughly, but did not discover the hiding place as the American soldier was well hidden in the cellar underneath the ruins of Henri's unused barn.

When Yvette returned, the American was agitated. "I need to get out of here. I need to find my friend. Thank you for what you have done, but I need to go now."

"No go. Good news. Friend is near. Coming here." Yvette said.

Raymond brought the other soldier to the barn. "He was found near Cécile's family's vineyard."

He told Yvette and the American. "We recovered much of the packages that they dropped from the plane before it crashed. The Germans were searching the plane, but since it was still burning, they left, thinking no one could have survived." Raymond's English was better than Yvette's.

The Americans were overjoyed to see each other. They were talking so fast to each other, Yvette and Raymond could not understand them. One soldier said to them, "We need to get moving. We need to radio London that we crashed and got out with most of the supplies. Do you have a transmitter?"

"Transmitter? *Oui.* Yes. Papa is operator. Come to house. Safe now. Germans gone." Yvette said.

Raymond helped to translate what the American soldiers discussed. They were impressed with Raymond's English. "Where did you learn to speak English so well?" One of the soldiers asked.

"I listen to American music. Frank Sinatra, Billie Holiday, Les Paul, Jazz, Glenn Miller. I sing along and play. I play guitar and sing the lyrics and learn English."

Jean-Paul returned with more of the supplies that were dropped. "The Germans saw a parachute come out of the plane before it crashed and are trying to find whoever or whatever landed. So I took the parachute and dumped it near the river with some of the broken debris. Hopefully they will think that the parachute landed in the water and will stop trying to look. There are guns, ammo, transmitters and money that was in the package. We recovered as much as we could."

They hid the supplies where the soldier had

slept, then went to Jean-Paul and Yvette's house. Henri had rabbit stew, wine, fruit and cheese for them. "You all must eat well because you never know where your next meal will come from."

"We are told you have a transmitter." said one of the soldiers. "We need to tell London what happened."

"Yes I know. I only transmit at seven o'clock in the evening, and only for a few minutes. The Gestapo have a way of locating signals if I transmit for too long. And you can't say anything that the Germans can understand." Henri explained.

"We know. We had to learn certain messages to send for a number of scenarios."

"Tell me the message and I will send it."

"This is what you are to send; *Dragon is on fire, the eggs have hatched.*" the soldier said. "I understand that we are also to use only our code names. I am Dragon." said Walter, "and this is Griffin." Walter said as he pointed to Theo.

Jean-Paul and the others introduced themselves also using their code names; Hawk, Raven, Camellia, Jasmine and Lilac.

"There is nothing more you can do until we get an answer from London." said Hawk. "You two will have to stay here until then. We must go and distribute the weapons and supplies that London sent us. We have someone watching the Germans. If they come near here again, you will be notified in time to go to the hiding place."

It was a couple of days later when the message came back. The soldiers could not be rescued until the next full moon. "I figured that would be the case." said Griffin.

Hawk told them that he knew of an

underground arrangement where Allied soldiers were sent to other Resistance Cells through France. They would be transported from one group to another until they crossed the Pyrenees Mountains into Spain. "It is a long and difficult journey. It may take even longer to get to Spain than if you stayed here until the next full moon landing. It is up to you both to decide what you want to do. Once you leave us, we will no longer know what happened to you. You might make it, or you might not."

Dragon and Griffin discussed their situation and decided to stay. "If we stay with you, what can we do to help? We can't just hide out for a month waiting for the next landing."

"If you want to help us, first you must take off your uniform. You can't go around here looking like American soldiers. We have some clothes that will fit you. I will take you to our camp where we will decide what we are going to do next." said Hawk.

One of the places that the Resistance group met was in a neighbor's abandoned barn. That family had evacuated with many of their neighbors when the Germans first invaded their area. When the nights were cold, they used as many different abandoned barns as they could, not daring to stay in one place too long. Henri sent them with food and bottles of wine that he had hidden from the Germans. After they ate, they discussed their next target and discussed with the Americans what they could do to help. Hawk explained how they became *Maquisards*. They heard that the Germans were taking young men from all over France and sending them to Germany to work in their factories. Many had no choice as their families were threatened if they did not go. The young men were told that they would be paid well and returned home later. But news got around that the men were sent to work in factories that made weapons to help kill their own countrymen. It was then that many young men took to the forests to hide out. There they knew that they could not return home as the Germans would find and punish them. There were so many men that escaped the work force, that they bonded together to fight the Germans. There were now so many *Maquisards* all over France, that no one knew how many or where they all were. An underground communiction system was set up that the *Maquis* could travel in and around the groups to exchange supplies and information about what each group was doing and the activities of the Germans. Raven told them how they started doing little things like cutting communication lines, derailing trains, and blowing up bridges. Then when they were able to get weapons from the parachute drops, they would ambush and shoot German soldiers.

Eventually some people became spies and counterspies. Some people would turn in their friends and family for rewards from the Germans. Raven told of one of their best leaders, Jean Moulin, who was caught, tortured and died in the German prison. They told the Americans how there were so many men wanting to do something but had so little supplies that they had to resort to guerrilla warfare. "When you return to London, you must tell Charles de Gaulle and the Allies how we need more if we are to rid our country of the enemy." Raven said.

They then spent some time teaching each other important words and phrases to know in their languages. Then Raven got out his guitar and started playing some of the French and American songs he knew. They all joined in on the singing. Dragon and Griffin taught them some of the latest American songs and Hawk and Raven and the other *Maquis* sang the *Marseilles*. The food, wine, songs, and the knowledge that the Allies would help free the French from German occupation gave them a feeling of camaraderie. They slept well that night.

Some of the supplies they had received, especially the cash donated by the Allies, the transmitters, and documents with information on the events going on outside of France, were to be delivered to various Resistance rendezvous areas around Paris. Dragon and Griffin were told they could accompany the women with the deliveries. Dragon would go with Camellia to Aubervilliers in the 19th arrondissement on the northern end of Paris, while Griffin would go with Jasmine to Boulogne-Billancourt in the 16th arrondissement in the southwestern end. They would take two different trains. They had false papers claiming them to be married couples, and identity badges called *Aussies*. If stopped, they would say that they were going to visit relatives in Paris. Jasmine had an aunt living in Paris, so the name and address they claimed they were going to was real. The aunt had evacuated to Biarritz where her children lived and her apartment was empty. Jasmine and Camellia knew where the key was and they were to go there after delivering the supplies to the Resistance. The deliveries were to be at certain restaurants and other places at predetermined days and times. These meeting places were always changing locations for safety reasons and because if anyone was caught, questioned, tortured, and broke, by the time the Germans got to the location, there would be no one there.

Dragon and Camellia walked hand in hand to the restaurant. They weren't paying attention as they should have been, so when they approached the restaurant, they were confronted by a German soldier. He was standing in the doorway as Dragon and Camellia were about to go in, the soldier demanded to know why they were going into the restaurant. "What is your business here? Show me your papers. We have arrested your friends who are all working for the Resistance."

Dragon was caught off guard, but Camellia was prepared. She knew that if Dragon spoke, the German would know that he was not French. She spoke up quickly, "We were going in for some bourbon. My husband has caught a cold and his throat is very sore. My mother told me that a shot of bourbon would help ease the pain, since we could not find any medicine. We have never been here before. Are those Resistance people really in here? We had no idea." Camellia tried to ramble on, distracting the German. One look at Dragon and her story seemed true as Dragon was white as a ghost. He didn't have to pretend to be sick.

It seemed an eternity that the German took to examine their papers. Camellia tried to look nonchalant as she squeezed Dragon's hand trying to signal him to remain calm. Finally the German gave their papers back. "One has to be careful these days as there are enemies lurking around. Be careful where you go. There's a place a few blocks down that should have some bourbon. You should stay inside from this awful weather so his cold will not get worse. Good day." He clicked his heels and turned away.

Dragon and Camellia walked away as quickly

and unobtrusively as they dared. They found a place in the park and sat down to catch their breath. Dragon said, "That soldier spoke French well. I could barely catch what you were telling him."

"Yes, many Germans speak French and other languages as well."

"I was so frightened. It is one thing to drop bombs on Germans not really seeing the enemy, but up close like that, it really hits home. I thought it best not to speak, but I could not have spoken anyway."

"You were very pale." Camellia said and started laughing.

Just then they were approached by an old gentleman who sat down beside them. *"Bonjour madame et monsieur. Je vous entends cherchez bourbon."*

"Oui, mon mari est malade." Camellia stuck to her story.

"Il fait plus froid dans les montagnes puis la ville," the man said, as he rubbed his hands together briskly.

Camellia knew this was the coded message and sign to use to identify that he was a Resistance contact. *It is colder in the mountains than in the city.* She turned to him relieved that she could trust him. She gave him the return answer, *"Je dois porter mes gants bruns,"* I should wear my brown gloves, with the sign of stretching her hands out in front of her, turning her palms up and down three times. She then told him that they had a package to deliver to the restaurant, but were confronted by the German soldier. "Was it true that they arrested those inside?"

"Yes." the man replied. "I was watching from nearby. I was also about to go inside to meet my contact, which I assume is you. I saw you talking with the SS soldier and was afraid you would be arrested too. You must have given the German a convincing story."

Camellia told the man what she told the German. "I wasn't sure how Dragon would react, so I had to talk quickly."

"Oh, so he is the Dragon and you are the Camellia that we heard about."

"You know about us?"

"Word gets around." he replied. "You must be careful with him. If it becomes obvious that he is American, well, I won't tell you how dangerous that could be. By the way, I am Fox. You have a package for me?"

"Yes," Camellia answered. "I'm glad you are here. I don't know what I would have done if I had to return with the package. It is so dangerous to have to make arrangements all over again."

Fox told her of another location to make the next delivery. He gave her a package to return to her village which contained the underground newspaper with news of what was really going on, and not the German propaganda that the French were fed. He also gave her coded messages about the German activities they were to send to London through WASP's transmitter.

All the while, Dragon was trying to understand what they were saying, he was aware that he and Camellia were still holding hands. It was a comforting feeling. He admired how brave she was in confronting the German. Thoughts of the war were gone as he watched her interact with Fox. He thought about the women he knew back home. None of them was anything like this Camellia. None of them would be as brave as she was, doing dangerous things because of her devotion to her country. The one woman he left behind was someone he had fun with, went to parties, to the beach, and dancing. But this one, this Camellia, she was mature. She had a passion. She was dedicated to a cause. He believed she would do anything for that cause. In fact, he realized that all the young Resistance members he met were like that. While he was flying planes for the exhilaration and danger, these people were fighting for something more important than that. They were fighting for their way of life, for their freedoms, for their country. He suddenly felt embarrassed by the fact that he was in this war for the excitement without thinking about what the war was really about. He realized how lucky he was growing up in a country with all the freedoms he had enjoyed, being able to live life as he pleased, while the young people of this country put their lives in danger every day to attain the freedoms he took for granted. That they would die for this gave him a feeling of insignificance. *I want to help these people,* he thought. *I want to do something that will make a difference. I want these Resistance people that I met to live and be free. I want Camellia to be free.* He then realized that he was squeezing Camellia's hand. She turned to him and gave him an odd look. *"Qu'est-ce que c'est?"* she asked. He was staring at her with such a sad expression, that she thought he was going to cry. *"Allons,* let us go." she got up quickly as she removed her hand from his.

"Oui, dépêchez." Fox said as he also got up.

On their way to the apartment belonging to Jasmine's aunt, they saw many Gestapo. Camellia knew the back streets they could take to avoid the

SS who were on the main streets. When they got there, Camellia found the key and let them inside. "*Ils ne sont pas ici.*" she said. "They not here."

Camellia tried not to look worried, but Dragon could see that she was. "It's ok. They'll be here soon." Dragon said to comfort her.

Camellia scrounged up what food she could find when Griffin and Jasmine arrived. "We brought some wine, cheese and baguettes." Griffin said. "Jasmine knew the people in the café nearby who had hidden supplies for people he knew."

"We were getting worried about you." Dragon said.

"Many German soldiers everywhere." said Jasmine. "*Je pense,* I think something happening."

"Your English is getting better." Dragon remarked.

"Griffin teach me more all day." she answered.

"How did your mission go?" asked Dragon.

"We accomplished our mission, but we encountered many German soldiers everywhere. We were able to deliver the ink and paper they needed to print more underground papers. We have copies of the *Resistance* to deliver to the people. They are printing it out of the *Musée de l'Homme.*" said Griffin.

After they ate, Camellia and Jasmine decided to go out to see what they could find out about what was happening, why there were so many more Germans everywhere.

"We will talk to friends of my aunt here in the building." said Jasmine. "You stay here. We will be back soon."

While they were gone, Dragon and Griffin talked about the situation they were in. "This is unbelievable." said Griffin. "We joined the war for excitement, and look what we got into."

"These people are so amazing." said Dragon. "I never knew anyone could be so loyal to a cause. They are fighting for a freedom that we take for granted everyday. So many are dying. We could die tomorrow."

"I hope we live long enough to get back to London. When we get back home, boy will we have stories to tell."

When the women returned, they did not look pleased. "What's wrong?" Dragon asked.

"My aunt's friend told us that the Germans are rounding up the Jewish people and deporting them to concentration camps. At first, they sent the Jewish families to Drancy in the northeastern area of Paris. The conditions there were deplorable, and some died. The rest were kept there for a while, but then the Germans started deporting them in trains to the concentration camps in Germany. The Jews are being told that they are going there to work, but many people think they are going there to be executed. She told us that one of the Jewish families nearby was taken away. Some of our people know what is happening, but they don't care. They are even encouraging the round-up and helping the Gestapo locate the families. They are taking men, women and children. They have no qualms about who they kill." said Jasmine.

"How do you know they are being executed in the concentration camps?" asked Dragon.

"There are spies and counterspies in the government. Many work there to gain information from the Germans and report to the Resistance what they find out. Some pretend to be friends of the Resistance, but report to the Germans our activities.

It is so difficult to know who to trust. I cannot believe some of our own people are helping the Germans." Jasmine answered.

"Should we return tonight to get this message to London?" asked Griffin.

"No. It is past curfew. We would certainly be caught." answered Camellia. "Besides, I think that London probably already knows what is happening."

"The Germans are exterminating the Jews, they are deporting our young men to work for them in their factories, who will be next? I fear for our country. Look how they have taken over the other countries they invaded. We must not lose. We cannot lose. You must return to London and tell them and the Allies to hurry up and free us. We are getting tired." said Jasmine.

Griffin took her in his arms and comforted her. Dragon put his arms around Camellia and told her that the Allies were doing the best that they could. "It will soon be over." Dragon said. "We know that the Allies have plans, but we do not know what those plans are. I think something will be happening soon."

"I hope soon." said Camellia.

"You and your friends are so brave. You must keep believing. We will do our best to get you the help you need in the meantime."

Dragon and Griffin wanted to take everyone's minds off of the war, so they asked the women to talk about their life and family. Camellia told about her father being in the first war and his injuries. "He suffered through one war, that is why he wants to do whatever he can to end this one. It was because of that war that we lost so much. My mother died because she was sick from hunger and was weak when she had me. So many people who worked on our vineyard died so my father could not keep it going like before."

Jasmine asked about America. "Tell us about your country. What do you do there? What is it like?"

Dragon and Griffin told them about their families and the beaches and the mountains and the parties and baseball games. "You would like it. Maybe when the war is over, you can come visit us."

"Yes. We would like to see America."

It was late into the night when they realized they needed to sleep. In the distance they could hear the sounds of the war. Gunshots constantly rang out. The odor of spent ammunition permeated the city and the apartment. Jasmine took Griffin's hand and led him to the bedroom. Camellia looked at Dragon and said, "We may not live through this war. Come with me. I would like you to hold me."

She led him to the other bedroom. At first Dragon held Camellia until he thought she was asleep. But she could not sleep, nor could he. She turned to him and they started cuddling and kissing. Then all the pent up emotions began to surface. The passion they felt was the most intense feeling Dragon had ever had. That first time was hurried, explosive and needy. All of their emotions were consumed in those moments of exquisite mania. They made love as if it were the last thing they would ever do because they thought any day would be their last. Exhaustion took hold and they slept for a few hours. As the early morning light crept into the window, they loved slowly and tenderly. Dragon felt a compelling desire to protect Camellia and take her away from this terrible war. He wanted this moment with her to last forever. He held her tightly, but she soon moved away. "We must go." she said.

When the four had returned from Paris, they immediately sent the message to London via WASP's transmissions about what was happening to the Jews. Then they delivered the underground papers, the *Resistance,* to various drop points around the area. Dragon and Camellia tried to sneak off whenever they could to resume their love affair, as did Griffin and Jasmine. It soon was no secret to the other members of the Resistance. Camellia's brother, Hawk, tried to talk to her, but she convinced him that she knew what she was doing. "When this war is over, Dragon will return. He will take me to America and we will be together."

"Provided we live through this." Hawk said.

"That's why we must grab hold of whatever life we can now. If we don't survive, then I will know that I lived life to the fullest. I love him now. I don't want to think about the future. Today, right now, is the only thing that matters. And today, right now, I am happy despite the war. Besides, it gives me more reason to keep fighting."

"Oh, Yvette, I wish things were different. We don't deserve to be in this war. We are in the prime of our lives. We should be having the time of our lives. Instead we are fighting a war we shouldn't have to be in. I want you to be happy I want you to have a wonderful future."

"And I want the same for you Jean-Paul." Yvette said as they hugged tightly.

In their forest hideout, the Resistance members were preparing for the next full moon pick up and delivery. Dragon and Griffin were anxious to be rescued and return to London to resume their air attacks. They were also sad to be leaving as they also wanted to stay with the Resistance and help them, especially Camellia and Jasmine. They had fallen in love with the women and were reluctant to leave them. They had already said their good-byes and went to the field to wait. They waited in the landing field for three days, but the plane did not come. They expected that as the weather was increasingly getting worse, but they had hoped the plane would come. The clouds were overcast and a cold drizzling rain was intermittently coming down. It would be another month before Dragon and Griffin could be rescued.

"There is still the escape route through France to Spain." Raven said.

"I think we shall stay here until the next full moon." Griffin said. "As you explained, it might take us longer than a month to get there, and there are too many unknowns, too many hands to slip through, too many dangers."

"Besides, we can be helping you." Dragon said. "We have done well together."

And so they stayed, continuing to go on missions with Hawk, Raven and the others.

CHAPTER ELEVEN

Late one night Dragon, Griffin, Camellia, Jasmine and Lilac were waiting in one of the abandoned buildings for Hawk and Raven and the others to return from a mission they went out on. It was five days that they waited and they were all getting worried. "Why are they not here yet?" said Jasmine.

"Maybe it is taking longer than they expected. You know they went to help blow up a bridge used to transport Jews to Germany. That is two days away. And it will be two more days to return. They are going to blow up the bridge just before the train gets there so that it cannot cross the river into Germany. Hopefully they are going to try to help as many Jews escape when the train is stopped." Griffin answered.

"I hope they did not encounter trouble. There are many Germans patrolling the route along the tracks." said Camellia as they were getting increasingly concerned. "Maybe we should go out and look for them."

"It is too dark now. If they are not back by morning, we will walk in that direction to see if we can meet them on their way back." Dragon said trying to comfort them. "Let's try to get some sleep. They'll probably show up during the night." Dragon and Griffin spread out the blankets on the cold barn floor, but none of them got any rest as their worry increased with each passing hour.

Early the next morning, they heard something outside the barn. "They are back." said Lilac as she hurried to the door.

"Wait." Griffin held her back. ""Stay here until I check it out. You don't want to come face to face with a German soldier."

They all stood silently as Griffin crept out the door to see who or what was out there. "Come quick," he yelled. "It is Raven and I think he is hurt."

They rushed to his side. Raven was dirty and there appeared to be blood on his clothes. He was trying to crawl towards them. Lilac knelt beside him. "Raven what happened? Are you hurt?"

Raven murmured something but they could not understand him.

"Raven, Raven what happened? Where are the others." Camellia begged as she looked around for them.

Raven was going in and out of consciousness, still babbling unintelligibly.

"Let's get him inside." Dragon said. "Help me carry him."

They laid him on a blanket and tried to give him some water. Dragon and Griffin tore off his clothes to see where the blood was coming from. Most of the blood was on his leg. There was a scarf tied around his upper leg like a tourniquet. Lilac cleaned the blood and found a bullet wound. "His leg is infected. It is red, swollen and hot to the touch." she said. "We must get him to a doctor."

"We cannot carry him all the way to town." said Jasmine. "I will go to the doctor and see if I can get something for him. "Camellia, can you and Dragon go get your father's cart so we can carry him to Lilac's farm? Lilac, you and Griffin stay with him."

Jasmine hurried into town and found doctor Lucian's office. She took a deep breath and tried to calm down before entering. "Doctor Lucian," she said trying not to look worried. She knew not to reveal why she wanted medicine because she did not know the doctor well enough to trust him. He could be with them, or he could be collaborating with the Germans. "Do you have something for an infection and fever?" she asked.

"And who might this be for?" he asked.

"Oh, my father has a small scratch that seems to be getting infected. I just want something to put on it so it doesn't get worse."

"Perhaps I should come out and see for myself." the Doctor said. "You can't be too careful these days.."

"Oh no. That won't be necessary. It's just a small scratch. You must have many more important patients to see."

They stared at each other, Jasmine beginning to feel panic, but trying hard to remain calm. *Why is he looking at me like that? Does he know something? Please just give me the medicine. Please. What will he say if he comes to my house and there is nothing wrong with my father?* Her thoughts raced through her mind as he kept looking at her. Then he put his arm around her and walked her to the cabinet.

"Here is some antiseptic and antibiotic. Be sure to clean the wound carefully, and give him this in case he has a fever." he said. Then he hugged her and whispered in her ear, "I heard a rumor that some of our local boys were helping other *Maquis* to derail a train some miles from here. Many were shot by the Gestapo. Be very careful. Take good care of him. We need good people like him to help us out of this mess."

"Yes, thank you. I will." she hugged him back. *What does he know? How does he know?* She felt a panic well up inside, but tried to walk slowly out of his office looking calm. Standing outside the door was a German soldier. She almost panicked, but had practiced enough to put on an act. *"Bonjour, monsieur."* she greeted the soldier with a smile.

The soldier looked at her, but said nothing. Instead he nodded, clicked his heels and turned away.

Jasmine arrived at the barn as the others were trying to put Raven in the cart. "Let me give him some medicine first." she said. "Has he said anything? The doctor knew about the bombing of the train. He said that the Gestapo shot many of the *Maquis.*"

"No, he is still delirious." said Camellia. "He just keeps babbling unintelligibly. We keep trying to talk to him, but he doesn't remain conscious enough to answer."

"We must get him to tell us what happened. Where are the others?" Jasmine pleaded.

After Jasmine cleaned his wound properly and got some antibiotic into his system, they slowly pulled the cart to Lilac's vineyard. It was the nearest to them as they did not want to travel too far with the condition that Raven was in, and the route would not take them on any main roads where they might encounter German patrols. Once they got him in bed, the women took turns taking care of him, putting cool rags on his head to break the fever, and giving him a dose of medicine when he was awake enough. It took another day before Raven was getting better, but he would awake and thrash around yelling, "No. No. No." Then he would look around as if not knowing where he was, and tried to get out of bed.

When he was awake, each woman tried to get him to talk. Camellia kept asking him, "What happened? Where is my brother? Where is Jean-Paul?" but all he would do is mumble.

Then, after becoming conscious enough to make sense, he told them he wanted everyone in the room. "We met with another Resistance group to blow up a bridge where the train carrying Jews to Germany would be passing through. We scouted the area carefully before going to set the fuses. We wanted to blow up the bridge just before the train got there because we wanted just the locomotive to derail and not the whole train. We didn't want the train to fall into the river because too many Jews would have died. We thought the derailment would cause enough commotion that we could shoot as many Germans as we could, then we would open the box cars and let the people out. I was one of the lookouts high on the ridge. I was to fire one shot if I saw any Germans nearby. I didn't see anyone. Then when Jean, I mean Hawk and the others went to the tracks and started to lay the fuses, shots rang out from everywhere. The Germans must have been well hidden. Someone must have told them of our plans. They shot everyone working on the tracks. Everyone. Then they fired everywhere, up on the ridges where the lookouts were, all around the train, and I think they even shot one of their own. Everyone is dead. I'm so sorry Yvette, Jean-Paul is dead."

"No. He can't be dead. No. Didn't you go to help him? What did you do? He might just be wounded. Didn't you go help him?" Camellia started shouting. "We have to go back, we have to find him. We have to go back."

"Tell us what happened. How did you get away?" Lilac asked.

"Like I said, I was on the ridge watching. They came out from nowhere. I didn't see them, so I never got to fire the warning shot, neither did the other lookout on the opposite ridge. When the German's started shooting everywhere, they didn't see me, but fired in all directions. That's when I got shot in the leg. I don't know what happened to the other lookout. I watched in horror as they shot everyone on the tracks. I fired shots at the Germans when they started firing everywhere. I think I got two of them. But I could see all of our men were down. There was blood and bodies all over the tracks. The Germans dragged them off the tracks and just left them there. Someone got to light a fuse, but it was too little to do any damage. He only got himself blown up. The train slowed, but was able to go on."

"Didn't you go try to help them?" Camellia was kneeling by the bed still shouting. Dragon tried to put his arms around her to comfort her, but she pulled away. "I need to see him. We need to go back and find him."

Jasmine knelt beside Camellia and said, "We need to hear the rest of the story. Let him finish."

"The Germans must have not seen me or the other lookout. I was behind some trees and bushes. When I got shot, I fired back, but I was losing a lot of blood. I tied a rag around my leg and crouched down. I covered myself with leaves. Some Germans came up on the ridge, but didn't see me. I stayed there for hours watching. I must have passed out from losing blood. When I awoke, I don't know how long I was out, but it must have been hours, there was no one anywhere. I don't know what happened. I don't know what they did with the bodies. I went down to the tracks. I saw blood trails leading to the river. I think they dragged the bodies to the river. I tried to find them, I tried. But there was no one. There was only this, Yvette, Jean-Paul's scarf. I used it to tie my leg to stop the bleeding."

Camellia took the bloody scarf and said, "Yes that is his scarf. Did you look everywhere? Maybe they got away while you were out. Maybe they are trying to get back here. We have to go look. We have to find them."

"No, there was too much blood. No one could have survived. Before I lost consciousness, I could see that no one was moving. They are all dead. I didn't see the German patrols. They are all dead because I didn't see the Germans. I didn't get to fire a warning shot." Raven lamented as he put his head in his hands.

"It's not your fault." Lilac tried to comfort him. "It's not your fault that you didn't see them. You should rest now." Turning to the others she said, "Let him rest. He is exhausted. Let him rest."

"No. No. I want to finish. I have to finish this." Raven took a sip of the soup Lilac gave him, then he continued. "The blood trails led to the river. I think the Germans dragged the bodies to the river. I tried counting how many trails there were. They are all gone. They all died and were dumped in the river. I followed the river to see if I could find anyone, but there was nothing. Someone's cap floating down the river, but nothing else. No guns, no clothing, nothing. I kept looking until I passed out again. I think I was able to stop the bleeding, but had lost so much blood that I could hardly stay conscious. I had to get back here, so I tried to make my way back. I don't know how long it took me to get back. What day is it?"

"I want to go there. Take me there. I need to find Jean-Paul." Camellia kept saying.

Dragon and Griffin looked at each other. "This is the first time they are using their real names. They are talking so fast that I can only catch a few words, but they are saying that everyone is dead. Jean-Paul must be Camellia's brother. He must be Hawk. Griffin said.

"I know. This is terrible if Camellia's brother is dead. I liked Hawk. He was a good leader. Should we try to help them find the bodies?" Dragon said.

"I don't think so. This is a war. Unfortunately people get killed. People we care about. There's nothing we can do."

"It was five days that we waited for you, then when you showed up, another two days before you regained consciousness. You left on the mission a week ago." Lilac told him. "Now you must get some rest." then she told the others, "Leave him."

Camellia was crying beside the bed. "No, please, tell me where Jean-Paul is. We must go find him."

Raven put Camellia's head on his lap and tried to console her. "I'm so sorry, Yvette. I tried. I failed. There was nothing I could do."

"No, please. No. No. No. We have to go back. We have to go back."

Dragon and Griffin went outside. They were angry. "Damn! Damn! Damn this war!" Dragon shouted. "These people don't deserve this! They are good people. Why did this have to happen to them?"

"It's happening all over this country. All these people just trying to live a normal life, and then some stupid, crazy, evil man wants to take it all for himself." Griffin said.

"They told us about these groups in training. It was just people all over the country trying to gain their freedom back. It meant nothing to us then. They were strangers. But now, they are people we care about. People getting killed. Young people who should be having a good time planning for their future. They should have the right to live as they please and not have to live secret and dangerous lives."

"We got into this war for the adventure and excitement. I never thought it would be like this."

"When we get back, we have to tell London. We have to get them to understand that we need to hurry up and get this war over with. This is sickening. I hate this. How many more innocent people have to die before the Allies get off their asses and help them?"

They went back inside. Lilac had given Camellia a sedative and put her in bed. Dragon wanted to stay by her side. He watched her try to sleep as he knelt by her bed. "I wish there was something I could do." He said softly.

Dragon had fallen asleep with his head on her bed. The others were in the kitchen each trying to cope with the sad news. Lilac's mother had made soup but no one could eat. Jasmine said, "We will avenge their deaths. We will shoot every German we see. We have guns and ammunition."

"I know how you feel." Griffin said. "But you must realize that that is the best way to get yourselves killed too. Dragon and I will go back to

London and tell them that they must speed up the process to free your country of Hitler's army. The Allies have a plan. I don't know what that plan is and I don't know what they are waiting for."

"If they don't hurry, there may not be any Frenchmen left. We have lost so many already." said Lilac.

Camellia woke to find Dragon holding her hand. At first, she was going to smile at him, but then remembered what had happened. She got up and started to cry again. Dragon woke up and held her. "What am I going to tell Papa? This will break him." she cried.

Raven had just awakened and tried to get out of bed. Lilac tried to get him to lay back and rest, but he objected. "I have to go. I have to find other *Maquis* and join them. I can't lie here while others are fighting." As he tried to get up, he fell.

"Your leg has not healed yet." Lilac said. "The bullet is still in it. We didn't take the chance of bringing the doctor here to remove it. We didn't know if he could be trusted. Maybe you should go to London with the American soldiers. You can tell de Gaulle what is happening and that we need more help. You can go to a hospital there and get better treatment."

"No. I'm not going anywhere. I'm going to keep fighting here. I know where other Resistance are hiding. I'm going to join them."

"Fine." said Lilac indignantly. "At least wait until you can walk."

Henri was sitting at the table sorting out the messages he had received from London when Camellia and Dragon entered. "I have more messages for you to deliver." he said, but when he saw the look on their faces, he knew.

"Oh Papa." Camellia ran into his arms. "I can't bear this. Jean-Paul is gone. They killed him."

Henri held Camellia for a long time. Dragon watched, feeling like an intruder. Then Henri asked Camellia, "Where is his body?"

Camellia tried to tell her father what Raven had said, but she couldn't bear telling him that the Germans dumped his body in the river and could not be found. She told him that Raven passed out from his injury and when he woke, the bodies were gone.

Dragon wanted to help Camellia explain so he said, "Hawk and his friends were very brave. I am so sorry."

Henri looked at Dragon. "*Merci.*" he said, "The message that I have from London is that they will send a plane to pick up you and Griffin. The full moon is in three days. I would ask you a favor."

"Anything, sir." replied Dragon.

"Take my daughter with you to London."

"No. Papa. I am needed here."

"I couldn't stand to lose you too. Please! Go to London. I'm sure there are things you can do there to help. Come back when the war is over."

"No. I'm staying here with you. My friends and I can still make documents and deliver papers. The Germans won't stop us. I don't have a gun and I won't be shooting at them, although I'd like to kill them all. I will be safe, Papa. I can't go to London. I can't leave you."

Dragon and Camellia spent the night at Henri's. Henri took Dragon aside and tried to convince him to take Camellia with them to London, but Dragon explained that there was only room for two people on the rescue plane. "I wish I could take her away from the horrors of this war," Dragon said, "and I'm so sorry about Hawk. He was a good leader. Everyone looked up to him and followed his lead."

"I understand. I went through this once already and lost many friends and family." Henri said. "I can't lose the only family I have left. Take her away from all this."

"I will do what I can, sir. Camellia is a strong and beautiful woman. I will come back for her as soon as I can."

They waited in the field again for the plane. It was the second night that they were waiting when they heard the engines. Dragon held Camellia tightly and told her, "I will return for you. Please be safe."

"I must stay with my father until this war is over. I will wait for you. Maybe someday you can take me and my father to America."

"I promise I will return. I want you to have my address in America. Write to me at that address and I will eventually get the letter no matter where they send me. I wish I didn't have to leave you like this. I love you, Camellia."

"We had wonderful moments together. I will never forget that. You helped me dream of things and take me away from this horrible war."

Dragon and Griffin got in the plane. As it took off, Dragon watched out the window at Camellia and the others. He watched as they disappeared below. "I love you Camellia." he whispered, "I will come back for you."

Camellia put the paper with his address in her pocket. She watched as the plane took off. She watched until it was out of sight. Her hand was holding the paper so tightly as if it was Dragon's own hand. "*Je t'aime mon cherie.*" I love you.

PART FOUR

CHAPTER TWELVE

Sophie read the letters over and over. She cried for her parent's lost love. She cried for the mother she never knew. She cried for her father not wanting her to know him while he was alive. She cried for the war. She cried for her adoptive parents having to keep the secret from her. She got angry at all of them for not wanting her to know. When her emotions were all spent, she went back to Cedric's office. "I hope there are no more secrets and surprises. I don't think I can take any more."

"No. No more secrets. Tell me what you are feeling. Do you have any questions?" Cedric asked.

"Yes. I have a million questions. Did they ever see each other again?"

"Sadly, no. It was more than three years before he got to go back to France to find her. You were three years old when he found you at the vineyard. He didn't know that your mother was killed until he got back to France."

"How did he find me?"

"Yvette had written him a letter telling him she was pregnant, but he didn't get the letter until the war was over. He didn't know that she was killed in the bombing of a train. Communications were spotty at best. During the war, many letters did not get out of France. The Germans intercepted and monitored all mail going in and out of France. Phones calls were also monitored. Only important calls were made.

Remember, that was in the 40's when there was no instant communication like there is today."

"So that is why it took three years to find me?"

"That, and the fact that the war was not over. He couldn't leave his postings. After they were rescued from France they were sent on other missions. Her letter was sent to his home address in New Jersey. His parents didn't think it was important, so they didn't send it to him. He didn't see it until he was discharged. Walter and Theo were shot down again over Germany and they both were wounded. This time they were caught by the Germans and sent to a prison camp. When the war was over, they were freed from the camp. Walter spent much of the time after the war in a hospital recovering from his wounds. He had to have his leg amputated and it took some time for him to get used to his prosthesis. It wasn't until he returned home that his parents gave him everything from the war. Stuff he had sent home, and Yvette's letter. That's when he was determined to return to France to find her and the baby. He was barely able to travel due to his injury, but he and Theo wanted to go back. Theo was in love with Jasmine and she was also pregnant. He didn't even have Yvette's address, and they weren't sure of their real names, but she did sign the letters Yvette. And they both knew they could find the vineyard where they were shot down."

"How did you know them?" Sophie asked Cedric.

"I was stationed in London, but I was not a pilot. I was a mechanic responsible for keeping the planes in working order. So I met with them when they were going on every mission. In between missions, we got to talking about planes and family back home and became friends. It wasn't until after the war when we met again and he told me about what happened in France. There wasn't much time for talking about adventures during the war and their involvement with the women. Our concentration was on our jobs and the reason we were there."

"If you were a mechanic, how did you become a lawyer?"

"My father was a lawyer. I was a mechanic because I had an interest in that, but after the war, many of us returned to school on the G. I. Bill. I wanted to be a lawyer like my father, so I went to school for that. Walter and Theo got government loans to continue in their parents' printing business. They both expanded their family's business after that and went into publishing. Walter and Theo later divided into different companies in different cities. As their businesses grew, Walter was able to send more money to your parents for your support.

"Tell me about how they found me. You said it was a vineyard near where the train was bombed. Who was the family that took care of me?" asked Sophie.

"I'll tell you what he told me about when they went to look for the women. This is the story of what happened when Walter and Theo returned to France."

CHAPTER THIRTEEN

Walter and Theo made their way to the vineyard where they met Camellia, Jasmine, and the other Resistance members. When they got to Henri's farmhouse, there was nothing there. The barn had burned down. There was no sign of Henri or Yvette in the main house. It looked as if it had been deserted for a long time. They looked through the house for any sign of its owners, or for any of Henri or Yvette's belongings. They found a couple of bottles of wine in a hidden place they knew about, but nothing else. Not knowing what to do next, they went to the neighbor's houses to see if they knew what happened to Henri and the other Resistance members. No one knew anything. They all said that when they returned after the war, that's all that was left.

Walter and Theo then went to the house where Lilac had taken Raven. "You are the American soldiers that were here when Jean-Paul was killed. We remember you." Lilac's parents said.

"Where is everyone? Where is Camellia, Jasmine, and the others? What happened to Henri's farm?" Walter asked.

Lilac's parents used the real names of the friends. "Yvette and Hélène and our daughter Cécile continued to work for the underground. They continued to make fake documents and deliver papers. Even when Yvette and Hélène were pregnant, they were able to hide things in their clothes. They were helpful in locating German strongholds and Henri sent vital information to London that helped the Allies know where to land and what to bomb. One day, the Germans were able to locate where the messages were being transmitted. They found Henri. We never saw him again. We didn't know if they killed him or took him away to their concentration camps." Lilac's mother said.

Cècile's father continued the story. "When Yvette, Hélène and Cécile saw what happened, they left more determined to continue their missions. So many of their friends and family had been killed or disappeared. Even after they had the babies, they continued to work for the Resistance. They spent much of that time in Paris. We didn't see much of them after that. Cécile returned one day to tell us that Yvette and Hélène were on a train to help with the rescue of Amiens prisoners when the train was bombed. Their babies were with them. No one survived."

"They are dead? Camellia and Jasmine and the babies are dead?" Theo and Walter were horrified. "That can't be! They sent us a letter saying that they were pregnant. We came back for them."

"We're so sorry. We didn't know you didn't know. We didn't know you would come back. Yvette and Hélène spoke fondly of you both. They hoped you would come back, but they didn't know if you would."

"Of course we were coming back. We wanted to take them to America. Especially after we found out that they were pregnant."

"There are many war time love stories. Not many of them work out after the war." said Cécile's father.

"Raymond and Cécile can tell you more about them. You should go talk to them." said Cécile's mother.

"Where can we find them?" asked Walter.

"They are in Amiens. They are at a café a couple of blocks from the cathedral. Cécile and Raymond both work at the café." said Cécile's mother.

Walter and Theo left the vineyard. "Damn. Damn. Damn the war. How could they be dead?" Walter yelled.

"It's so unfair. They were beautiful and so devoted to their cause. They wouldn't have harmed a fly. Who killed them and why? We must find out. I'll kill the bastards that did this!" exclaimed Theo.

As they walked around the cathedral looking for the café, they heard singing coming out of the one they were passing. "That sounds like Raven. Remember how good a voice he had?" said Theo.

They entered the café and sat by the window listening to Raven sing. Memories came back of the days they spent in the woods with the Resistance. Suddenly they were approached by the waitress. "*Puis-je vous aider?*" she said. Then she stopped and shouted, "Dragon? Griffin?"

"Lilac!" They both exclaimed together. They got up and hugged her. "That's Raven singing?"

"*Oui!* Yes! What are you doing here?"

"We returned to find Camellia and Jasmine. We saw your parents. They told us what happened and where to find you. Please tell us what happened. Tell us that was a mistake that they are not dead." said Walter.

"*Ce est vrai.* It is true. *Je suis désolé.* We are so sad. So many of our friends are dead. Come.

Raymond and I will tell you everything."

Raymond did not seem particularly pleased to see them. "We did not think you would come back. It was so long ago."

"Three years is not that long. Anyway we could not come until the war was over. Then I spent time in the hospital. As you can see, I lost my leg." Walter said.

"You should have taken them with you in the plane to London."

"You know we could not. I wish to God we could have taken them with us." said Theo.

"Will you tell us what happened?" said Walter.

"Let us go upstairs. I'll bring some coffee. We will tell you what we know." said Cécile.

Raymond began, "After Jean-Paul died, I went to join another Resistance group that I had contact with. I was determined to kill all the Germans that I could. But my leg never healed right. The bullet is still inside. During one of our missions, the Gestapo must have been informed of our operation and again we were surprised. Most of us got away, but because of my injury, I could not run as fast. I was captured with a couple of others. We were sent to Amiens Prison. There were hundreds of us there. Many of the prisoners were important Resistance leaders and some Americans too. The Allies found out that many of us were going to be executed soon and they thought it was important to free us, so one day they sent Mosquito Squadrons to bomb a hole in the outside wall so we could escape. It was called Operation Jerico. Many were killed, but many did escape. I was fortunate to have escaped, but my time there caused my injury to worsen because they did nothing to help the sick and injured."

"What does that have to do with Camellia and Jasmine?" asked Theo.

"Yvette and Hélène knew that I was in Amiens to be near Raymond." said Cécile. "They were in Paris when they got the news. I was helping to arrange for escape vehicles. Yvette and Hélène were to take a train to meet me. On the way, the train that they were on was bombed. We knew that they were on that train. We hoped that they missed it, but when they never showed up, we knew something was wrong. We never saw them after that, so we assumed that they were killed along with everyone else on that train."

"The train was bombed near Amiens." said Raymond. "Perhaps you can go there and talk to the villagers."

"Tell us more about Yvette and Hélène. Tell us about the babies." Theo wanted to know.

"How did you find out about the babies?" Cécile asked.

"Yvette wrote to me. I didn't get the letter until I got out of the hospital. My parents kept all my belongings until I was discharged. That's when I discovered her letter. She told me she was pregnant. I wanted to return to take her to America, even if there was no baby. We both vowed to come back for them." said Walter.

"What can you tell us about the babies?" Theo asked.

"After you left, we wanted to do more to help. We continued to deliver documents. Then when Yvette and Hélène discovered that they were pregnant, they were then able to do even more." said Cécile.

"How could they do more in their condition?"

asked Theo.

"Their pregnancy gave them an even greater way to hide documents. They even rode on trains with the Germans. They told the Gestapo that the babies they were carrying were German. So they were treated well by them. They were even privy to important information that they relayed to the Resistance. The same was true after the babies were born. They told the Germans that the fathers were killed and then the Germans took even better care of them."

"When were the babies born?" asked Walter.

"It was December. They spent a lot of time in Paris at Hélène's aunt's apartment. The babies were born there."

Walter and Theo looked at each other with knowing looks. They both knew that that was most likely where the babies were conceived. "Didn't they go to a hospital?" Theo asked.

"No. They knew one of Hélène's aunt's friends was a midwife. She delivered both of the babies. I think Hélène's was born a few weeks before Yvette's." Cécile said.

They sat around the table for a while not saying anything, each in their own reminiscing. Finally Raymond lamented, "All of that, the war, the deaths, all because some psychotic idiot wanted to rule the world. Why did so many of my friends die? Why did I survive?"

Cécile comforted him. "You did survive. There must be a reason for that. Maybe it is to tell the story to others."

"You have a special gift of music." said Walter. "I remember when we were back in the forest when we sang your French songs and we taught you some

American tunes, you played the guitar and sang beautifully. You even made up some lyrics. You are using that gift now to entertain people. We heard you singing when we came into the café."

Why don't you sing them the song you wrote for Hawk?" said Cécile.

"What song is that?" asked Theo.

"Raymond had written a song to remember Jean-Paul. He sings it here often. Many people come here to listen to him sing. He does have a wonderful voice. Raymond, sing it for them." Cécile said.

"No. not now." Raymond said.

"We'd like to hear it. We admired Hawk. We liked him and were sad when he was killed. We have also lost many friends in the war." Theo said.

"It seems as if it was yesterday that we all were together, yet it was an eternity ago." Walter commented.

"Yes, it was an eternity ago, a different time and a different place. And we were different people then. We had a purpose, a goal, a meaning to what we did every day, a reason to fight." said Cécile. "Now that goal is accomplished, we are liberated, we have our freedom back, our country and our lives."

"What good is all that when we don't have our friends and family to share it with? What are we to do now? It seems that we have no purpose anymore." lamented Raymond.

"There is a purpose. We must work to rebuild our country from the damage. We must go on and live our lives in memory of our friends. Jean-Paul, Yvette, Hélène, the babies, our families and friends in the Resistance. We must live the lives they gave theirs for. They would not want us to do anything differently." Cécile said.

"You are right, Cécile. I'm sorry for feeling this way. You always help me out of my sadness." Raymond said.

"Perhaps it is time to go downstairs. The people want to hear you sing. Maybe you would sing Hawk's song for them."

They went downstairs to the café where Raymond began to sing. Walter, Theo and Cécile listened with tears in their eyes as Raymond sang his tribute to Hawk, each with their own memories of their time together in the war.

Velvet wings of the Hawk
soar above the clouds
wrapped around the moon
Night shadows evaporate
Hawk has flown away
as fire rises from the river
Raven's wing has broken
while searching for the path
surrounded in darkness
leading the masses
through the churning rivers
across the mountain peaks
in the shadows of the forest
and the ashes of broken cities

I am Raven
Fly with me
lonely followers
Across the roads
through the twisted crosses
in the darkest of our days
though the flowers have wilted
their aroma remains

in the secret shadows
of our hearts
Memories of Freedom
will guide us
until Raven turns white
and morning rises
when Hawk returns
to take us home

Cécile thanked the soldiers as they left. "Where will you go now?" she asked.

"There is nothing left for us here." said Walter. "We will go back home."

"Maybe you should go to the village near Amiens where the train was bombed." said Cécile. "The people there can show you the graves, and maybe tell you what they know about the wreckage."

"I don't know if I can handle any more sadness." Walter said.

"You can show your respect for them, maybe say a prayer. Put some flowers on their graves for me?"

"I suppose we could go there." said Theo. "We will probably never return to France. It might help if we see where they are buried."

Cécile gave them the directions to the village outside of Amiens and thanked them again. "I think you have helped Raymond by remembering the reasons we were together before. He has been so down since the war was over. Maybe he can begin to recover as we rebuild. I hope you both will recover too. I am so sorry for all the friends we lost. Here is also the address of my parents if you ever want to write to me. I'd like to know how you are both doing.

I will never forget you Americans. You do not know how grateful we all are for your help. Good luck to you both. Come back someday." She kissed them both on their cheeks and hugged them as if she would never let go.

The mayor was sitting at his desk when the two men came in. "*Bonjour messieurs. Puis-je vous aider?*"

"Do you speak English?" Theo asked.

"*Oui.* Yes. You are Americans? What can I do for you?"

"We'd like some information about the train that was bombed near here during the war. It was on the way to Amiens Prison."

"Yes, I remember. What would you like to know?"

"There were two women with babies on the train. Can you tell us what happened to them." Walter asked.

"Why are you interested in them?" asked the Mayor.

"We think we know who they were. Please, if you know what happened, where they are buried, we would like to visit the graves."

"We buried everyone in a separate cemetery from ours, since they were Germans. I'll take you there. On the way, you can tell me how you came to know those women."

As they walked to the cemetery, Theo told the mayor about how they were pilots delivering supplies to the Resistance when they were shot down. He told him that they were rescued by a Resistance group and the women were members of that group.

The mayor looked concerned as he showed

them the graves. "You knew the women? They were French? We didn't know who they were. The train was full of German soldiers so we assumed they were German women. We buried all the bodies in this separate cemetery because we didn't want the Germans in our cemetery. How do you know that these women were the ones you knew?"

Theo explained to the Mayor that they had just returned to find the women, and the Resistance members told them that they knew the women were on that train.

"Why would French women be on a train with German soldiers?" he asked.

"They were involved in clandestine activities, gathering information to send to London. They were on their way to Amiens Prison to help the other Resistance members who were planning to transport the freed prisoners." Walter said.

"Oh, my. Then we will have to move their remains to our cemetery. We don't want our Frenchmen buried with the Germans. Here are the graves." The mayor pointed out the three burial plots.

Walter and Theo looked surprised. "Why are there only three graves? There are two for the women and one for a child. Where is the other child buried?"

The mayor looked at the men curiously. "One of the babies survived." he told them.

Walter and Theo were shocked at the news. "One of the babies is alive?" they said. "Where is he? What did you do with him?"

The mayor asked them, "Why are you so distressed about these women and the babies?"

Theo told the Mayor their story. "We fell in love with the women. The babies were ours. We didn't know they were pregnant until we were discharged and sent back home after the war. They sent us letters. We came back to take them to America. We didn't know they were killed until we returned and found the other Resistance members that told us what happened."

"I'm so sorry. Let's go back to my office and I will tell you about the baby. You can tell me who these women were so we can contact their families. There was no way for us to know who they were. There was so much devastation to the train, we were surprised that there were any survivors. There was the wreckage, the sirens, the fires and the screams. The baby could have belonged to anyone. The few German soldiers who survived claimed not to know about the women and any identification they might have had on them was burned." The Mayor told them the story of how the villagers went to the wreckage and tried to help in any way they could. The baby was found alive with minor burns. "I think that her mother heard the bombs and tried to shield her baby under the seat of the train. That is the only way she could have survived."

"The baby is a girl? Where is she? We want to see her."

The Mayor struggled with what to do next. He frowned as he explained. "The family that has her thought that we would never find out who she belonged to. They took her in and raised her as their own. She is part of their family now. Their young daughter has the responsibility of taking care of her as the rest of the family works to rebuild their land. The girl loves her like a sister. The family lost a son in the war, and the baby has been a delight to them."

"The baby belongs to us." Walter said angrily.

"Walter, wait." Theo said. "We have to think about this. What are we going to do with a baby?"

"I don't know and I don't care. The baby is ours."

The Mayor interrupted. "Your friend is right. You have both been through a lot and this is more overwhelming news to deal with. The war, the deaths of your friends, your injuries. Take some time to think about this. Besides I would have to talk to the family first and prepare them for the news. Stay here tonight. There are rooms above the café in town. I will set you up there and we will talk more tomorrow."

Walter and Theo waited impatiently for the Mayor to return the next morning. "The family has agreed to speak to you, but there are no guarantees about what you will learn, or what they will agree to do. They are very attached to the child." The Mayor explained. "They want to know the truth, but realize that the truth may cause them to lose the child. They understand what is at stake. Try to understand their position."

The Mayor helped translate the conversation between the Americans and the Ducros family as neither spoke each other's language well. Madame Ducros told of the events of that day. "When we heard the sirens, we went to the cellar. But the sound was different. We knew that it was much more than the regular sound of a train whistle. Then we heard the bombs and the sounds of explosions and knew that the train had been bombed. When we thought it was safe, we went to the wreckage. In the devastation we heard the cries and screams and knew there were survivors. Our neighbors were already there trying to see what they could do. Then we heard the sound of a baby crying. We found her under a woman who was dead. There was rubble on top of them which I think was what saved the baby. If we had not gotten there when we did, I think the baby would not have survived much longer, even though she had minor injures, it was very cold and she was freezing. We let our daughter, Dominique take her back to the house and care for her while we continued to help with the other survivors."

"Can you describe the women?" asked Theo.

"No." said Monsieur Ducros. "They were too badly burned. Besides we were trying to help those who were alive."

The Mayor then said, "We can talk to the others who helped. Maybe someone else can tell you more. There were others who buried the bodies. Maybe they can describe the women."

The townspeople were reluctant to talk about it at first, but when the Mayor explained to them who the Americans were and why they wanted to know what happened, eventually the people came to the Ducros house and each one told his or her story about that day. Walter and Theo did not learn much more, but were thankful to the people who offered their help. The townspeople thanked Walter and Theo and told them how grateful they were to America and the Allies for helping them rid their country of the evil occupiers.

During this time Walter and Theo got in touch with Cedric and told him of their dilemma. They wanted to know what needed to be done for them to take the child to America. Cedric told his father who was a lawyer and the paperwork was started.

Walter and Theo visited the Ducros family

every day to see the child. At first the baby was hesitant, but with each visit, she warmed to the American soldiers. Dominique however did not. She knew that they were going to take her baby away and she hated them for that. She felt sorry for the soldier that lost his leg and was grateful for the Americans who helped her country, but her love for the baby and the thought of losing her was foremost in her mind. Her mixed emotions fueled her nightmares.

Finally the documents and paperwork were ready. Cedric's father had done a remarkable job in getting them in order for Walter and Theo to take the child to America. The day came when they went to the Ducros house to get the baby.

Dominique was with her out in the vineyard hoping to delay the inevitable. Madame Ducros had to call her a number of times before Dominique reluctantly brought the child inside.

"Are her things packed?" asked Theo.

"*Qui.*" Dominique answered. "I go get them." Dominique went upstairs where she added her favorite book, *Le Petit Prince,* and one of the photos taken of her family. She hid the photo inside the cover of the book hoping one day the baby would find it and remember her.

They had all said their good-byes, Dominique being the saddest as they took the baby away. She watched through the upstairs window until she could no longer see the car driving them away.

Walter and Theo were also reluctant to take the baby away, but decided that the baby belonged with them. "I hope Cedric's father has everything arranged." Theo said.

"I think we're doing the right thing. The baby belongs in America." Walter remarked.

"The Ducros are good people. They would have taken good care of her." Theo said.

"But they are not her real family. We can be sure she has the best of everything. France is still recovering from the war, I don't think that is the best place for her to grow up." Walter said.

"Cedric got in touch with our cousin. He said it is all arranged. We will meet with them when we land. They are good people. Later when we get our lives together, we can decide to take her to our family and raise her."

"I hope that will not be too long from now. She is so beautiful. She must have the best of everything. Until we can give her that, it is best for her to be with the St. Pierre's. They have tried to have a child for so long. They are excited to take care of her until we are able to."

CHAPTER FOURTEEN

Sophie was staring out the window of Cedric's office. "How did I end up being adopted?" she asked him. "If they wanted me raised in America, why didn't they keep me? Why did they put me up for adoption?"

"It was decided while they were in France. They wanted you to have the best, but they did not have a chance to marry the women and besides had no means to raise you. Also remember that was in the 40's and having a child out of wedlock was unacceptable. Walter's cousin, your adoptive mother, was unable to bring a baby to full term, so when they contacted her, she her husband readily agreed to raise you. Walter and Theo didn't plan for you to stay with them forever, but as time went on, they never found the right time to tell you the truth and take you back. You were getting the best of care with the St. Pierre's. Walter and Theo's parents were strict religious people and they felt they could not tell them about the baby. They figured they would find a way to tell them later."

"So their families never knew about me?" Sophie asked.

"I discussed the idea of your grandparents raising you, but they felt that their parents would not accept that they had affairs with French women and a child was the result of that affair. They did the best that they could under the circumstances."

"Then their families never knew about me? I was their dirty little secret?"

"No. Sophie, don't think like that. They loved you very much and thought their plan was the best they could do for you. They were just back from a terrible war. They were injured and thought they had nothing to offer you at the time. Please try to understand how things were then. Life was difficult enough after a war. And to have a baby to raise would have made it all the more difficult."

"You said they were going to tell me at some point? Why didn't they?"

"Walter and Theo returned to their parents' printing business. Eventually they did well, improved the business to publishing and branched off to different cities. It was years before they started making money. By then, everyone had started a new life and involving their new families and your adoptive parents would have been traumatic for all involved."

"They both got married?" Sophie asked.

"Yes. Walter married a woman who loved him very much. He may not have loved her like he did your mother, but she was devoted to him. As you know, Walter could not have children after the war due to his injuries, but they had a good life. Theo also married and had children."

"Did they ever tell their wives about me?"

"I don't believe they did. As I said, they were doing well and they knew you had the best of everything. Your life was good. They were satisfied that they made the right choice, and as time went on, it would have been more difficult to reveal the truth. I think at some point they decided it would be better not to tell you the truth."

"Then why now?"

"Walter's wife died of cancer a few years ago. He became desponded and thought of you more and more often. You were his only family. His parents died long ago, and when your parents died, he decided he wanted to leave you something of himself because he knew that you had no other family and he didn't like to think that you would be alone. He wanted you to have his house and a share of his company. Since he couldn't have children after the war, he involved himself in yours. He attended all your important functions that he could so he could see you. He was at your graduation and many other times where there were lots of people he could mingle with and not stand out."

"Why didn't he contact me after my mother died? It seems that would have been a good time to tell me."

"He thought about it, but after his wife died, his health went downhill. He didn't want you to see him like that. He thought you would feel sorry for him so he decided not to tell you then."

"Maybe I could have been some comfort to him."

"I tried to talk to him, but he wouldn't listen. He was stubborn. I was his lawyer and had to follow his orders or I would have contacted you myself."

This company that he built, It mentions Hawthorne Publications. Isn't that the company that owns *The WorldView?*"

"Yes. Walter was CEO of Hawthorne Publications. *The WorldView* was one of their divisions. That was his most successful venture." Cedric knew where this was leading so he told her.

"And yes, he was responsible for your getting the job with them. He informed Doris and Len to watch over you while you worked for them."

Once again Sophie was shocked. "Oh, my God! You mean that I was offered the job because he wanted me to work for him?"

"Yes you were offered the job because of him. But you didn't have to take it."

"Oh, so my whole career was based on a lie? My whole life was based on a lie? The children's book that I received an award for that he published, it was because I was his secret daughter? What else are you going to tell me?" Sophie got up as if she were going to leave.

"Sit down, Sophie. Let me explain." Cedric tried to calm her down.

"What's to explain? I would not be where I am today if I didn't have his help pushing me toward success after success!"

"That's only partly true. You were offered the job with Doris and Len. You didn't have to accept it. You could have gotten married instead as you were planning to do. He would have supported that too. He only wanted to give you everything you wanted. He only wanted you to be happy."

"But I had an advantage no one else had."

"Doris saw after the first assignment in Alaska that you had a talent for photography and reporting. She felt that you learned quickly and were not afraid of unexpected things that occurred like the earthquake and tsunami. You showed that you were brave and could handle situations. They were told to offer you another assignment and you took it. You developed the skills on your own, and yes with the help of Doris and Len. Len didn't want to help you at first, but he came to admire you. Len had to move up the ladder the hard way. He still resented you for having been given the opportunity that he had to work so hard for. But he did see that you had talent."

"That's why Len was always so distant. He didn't like the fact that I was handed life on a silver platter."

"Doris was also reluctant. She had to work hard to get where she was too. And having a secret life hiding the fact that she was gay. It was uncomfortable for her. Walter convinced them that it would only be a one time assignment, that you would probably go back home after Alaska and get married. But when they all saw how good you were and could become, Walter told them to offer you another assignment and you kept on accepting."

"My life was manipulated by Walter."

"Some of it, yes. But as I said, it was your choice to continue. You could have said no."

"I don't know if I can accept what he is leaving me. I did nothing to earn it. I didn't even have the opportunity to get to know him. He stayed informed and involved in my life, but he denied me the right to know him." Sophie was still upset as she thought about all that was revealed to her in the last few weeks. "As a lawyer, don't you think I had a right to know? Didn't any of you think about what I would have wanted? When I was offered the position at *The WorldView,* didn't any of you think that would have been a good time to tell me? Then I could have made my own decision. I wouldn't feel as though I was manipulated."

"Sophie, listen." Cedric took her hands in his as he explained. "I understand that you are upset.

But think of this before you make a decision. I want you to think of your biological mother. You read in Walter's letter how much he loved her. They only spent a couple of months together, but she was all he talked about. When he returned from that mission, all he could think about was returning to France to be with her and bring her to America. All he talked about was his French Camellia and how she would love America. He saw the devastation of her country and wanted to give her anything to make her happy. He was devastated when he found out she was killed. That only made him love her more. She gave her life for her country, for her beliefs, and freedom for her people. Your mother never got the chance to live a normal life, get married and raise a family. Think of the life she never got to have. Live your life for her."

"You are right, Cedric. I'm sorry I was only thinking about myself. There is so much to think about, so much I learned here. I have to process all this before I make any decisions."

"You had a good life. You were loved by everyone. Your adoptive parents could not have loved you more even if you were their biological child. Walter loved you. The life he planned with your mother was taken from him in the war. He was sad and depressed. You were all he had to remember her by. He wanted you to have everything that he promised to your mother. Her life was hard during the war. He wanted her to come to America and enjoy the freedoms here. But when she died, he felt that he let her down. He tried to make up for that loss by giving you everything."

"I don't know where to go or what to do. I feel kind of lost. How do I make sense of all this?" Sophie asked herself outloud.

"Take your time. There is no need to make a decision now. Take a week, a month, however much time you need. In fact, I have an idea. Why don't you go to France? Why don't you find the place where your mother grew up? Go to that village and find someone who knew her. Go visit the town near Amiens where the train was bombed. Find the people who took you in for three years. I think they would be happy to see you again."

"You mean you know where they are?" Sophie asked.

"Yes, even more than that. When Walter took you away, he promised them he would write to them and tell them how you are doing. He saw how much they loved you and was touched by their concern. Through the years, we sent them pictures and stories about your life."

"Oh, more surprises. Then they knew what happened to me? More people knew about my life then I did." Sophie scoffed.

"That may be true, but it shouldn't affect what you do next."

"I will think about going to France. I feel so overwhelmed. Maybe I'll go home to New Orleans where I at least feel at home. I have taken enough of your time. I need to go. I'm sorry for taking up so much of your time."

"Not at all. I've been involved with this for so long that I feel I know you as well as my own daughter. Walter, Theo and I have remained friends all these years and he always talked about you and about how proud he was of you. Sometimes he was sad because you reminded him of Yvette. I think that's why he could not bring himself to tell you of her. That would have brought up memories he could not deal with. He never got over losing her and what might have been."

"That is so sad. Maybe I could have been a comfort to him all those years."

"Maybe so, but what is done is done. You have to look to the future now. Call me anytime if you need anything or just want to talk. I'll give you the information you need to find the places in France that you ought to visit. I also have a corporate jet to fly you there. Let me know what you need."

"Thank you, Cedric. I'll be in touch soon. Good-by."

Instead of going home, Sophie decided to pay a visit to her friend and mentor, Doris. Sophie realized she hadn't seen her in a few years and felt bad about that. She knew that Doris' health was declining since her retirement and she should have visited her more. Sophie wasn't sure if she should confront Doris or not talk about what she knew. She didn't want to upset Doris.

Marge answered the door. "Sophie. How nice to see you. Please come in. Doris is in the living room resting." Marge led Sophie to where Doris was. "Doris, look who came by to see you."

"Sophie, sweetheart. Come sit by me." Doris said weakly.

"Doris. I'm sorry to bother you. If you're not feeling well, I won't stay long."

"No, stay a while. I don't get many visitors. It's so good to see you. How have you been?"

Marge brought them some tea and while offering Sophie some, she looked scornfully at Sophie. "It's time for you medicine Doris."

Sophie started to make small talk, but Doris

interrupted her, "Get to the point Sophie. I don't have the energy for idle chat."

Startled, Sophie asked, "What do you mean?"

"Cedric called. He told me everything. He said you might be coming by to ask me questions."

Sophie was taken aback. Tears welled up as she said, "I'm sorry Doris. I'm just so confused. I know none of this was your fault. You were just doing what you were told to do. I'm not here to blame you. I just wanted some answers. But it doesn't matter now. If you're not feeling well I shouldn't be bothering you about my dilemma."

"I think you already know the answers. Yes Len and I were sent to New Orleans to hire you. It wasn't just a chance meeting at the *Times Picayune*. It was all a set up. Walter wanted us to take you on the assignment to Alaska to give you the opportunity to see what it was like to be a journalist. It was just going to be a simple trip. Then the earthquake and tsunami happened. We were all impressed with how bravely you handled it. You didn't whine or panic. You jumped right in. You even said on the way home that it was the most exciting and scary thing you ever encountered."

"Yes, I remember. It was exciting. It's hard to believe that it was so long ago. Thinking about it now, it seems like it was just yesterday." Sophie recalled.

"After we returned, when we saw your photographs and stories you wrote about the children, Walter was impressed so he told us to ask you to go on the next mission with us. We all thought you would probably say no and get married instead. But you didn't. You accepted the offer. After the next few assignments, we assumed that you wanted to keep on doing this, that you were becoming dedicated to Journalism and didn't really want to marry that boy. So we were told to offer you a job permanently."

"And I said yes. I was so excited to think that I was good enough to work for a major magazine. I never thought I was handed the job on a silver platter."

"You were good enough. Don't think that just because you were given the opportunity that you didn't deserve it."

"Len didn't think I deserved it. He never really liked me, did he?"

"Len was against the idea. But he knew where his paycheck was coming from. Cedric told you that both Len and I had to work hard to get where we were. Then you come in and get it all without having to climb up the ladder. Of course we both resented you at first. But you learned fast and you showed us all that you were good. Eventually Len came to admire your work, but he never could get close to you."

"What happened to him?" Sophie realized she lost track of Len and never asked about him.

"He went on to Vietnam to photograph the war there. He was killed in a sniper attack." Doris said.

"Oh, that is so sad. I guess since he was so standoffish I never got to thank him for all that I learned from him. I should have been more concerned and involved with your lives."

"Don't worry about that. Len knew that you appreciated his help. You were young and excited and learning about life. That's what young people do."

Marge interrupted the reunion. "Doris, you

need to rest. Sophie, I hate to break up your reminiscing, but it's past time for Doris to take her medicine and she needs to rest."

"Bah! That's all I do is rest." Doris said.

"Really, I should be going now. Thank you Doris. I guess there was nothing you could tell me that I didn't already know. I am just so overwhelmed I didn't know what to do next. I felt that my life was all manipulated and I wonder if any of it was my choice."

"Of course it was. So what if you were given a head start. If you are handed an opportunity, take it. You took it and made the most of it. Don't ruin it with some philosophical idea that you are not in control. This is a turning point in your life. Cedric told you to go to France and discover your heritage. I think you should do just that. Go and make a great adventure of it. What you do is always your choice. Or you can stay here and do nothing but mope about being manipulated. You decide."

CHAPTER FIFTEEN

Sophie looked out of the window of the plane as Paris came into view. It was just past midnight and the City of Lights was sparkling. She tried to locate the Eiffel Tower as the plane decended on Charles de Gaulle International Airport.

I'm really going to do this, she mused. *I'm going to meet strangers who knew my parents and maybe find someone I am related to. Will my presence remind them of a time that they wish to forget? Or will I be welcomed.*

In the hotel, Sophie took out the map that Cedric had given her. She traced the route from Paris to the city of Amiens and the small town near there where her mother was killed. Cedric told her that the townspeople buried the victims in a special cemetery. If she decided not to visit the Ducros family, she could at least visit the grave site and pay her respects to her mother. Cedric wanted to call the family to tell them that she was coming to visit, but Sophie told him not to do that because she wasn't sure if she wanted to see them. She didn't want to be held to a promise that she might not keep. She reasoned to Cedric that it would be an even better surprise if she showed up unexpectedly.

She hardly slept on the plane, but wasn't feeling jet lag yet. As morning dawned, she left the hotel to tour Paris with the intention of taking her mind off of what she was going to do the next day. She rode the Metro to the Louvre hoping to be distracted by the art, but found herself wondering if her parents had ever been there, especially her mother since she lived in France. *I don't know anything about my mother's life,* she thought. She crossed the Seine and walked down the Champs Élysées but again thought about if her parents had walked this same street. *Everywhere I go all I can think of is if they came this way, or saw this or went there.*

Exhausted, she returned to the hotel, tried to enjoy eating her first French meal, then slept until the next morning. Still not sure of her intentions, she put her suitcase in the rental car and started driving North out of Paris towards Amiens. Arriving in the city, she found Notre Dame Cathedral, parked and went inside. There she found a war memorial, but it was for the First World War. It was a memorial to the Australians who died there defending the city. *So many people died in both wars helping to save this country,* she thought.

Next to her was an elderly couple who were also reading the names on the plaque. Interestingly, the man was speaking to his companion in English. Sophie turned to them and asked, "Are you Americans?"

"Yes we are." the woman answered. "It sounds like you are too."

"I am." replied Sophie. "I'm from New Orleans, but have a place in New York. My name is Sophie St. Pierre."

"We're from South Carolina. I'm Gloria and my husband is William. We are the Linkletters. What are you doing in Amiens, if you don't mind my asking?

This is an out of the way place for most tourists."

Sophie didn't want to tell strangers why she was here, so she answered, "I'm just visiting out of the way places too. I'm a photographer and I like to take photographs that are different from the usual."

"That's very nice," Gloria said. "Would you mind taking a photograph of us standing in front of the cathedral?"

"Of course. That's a very good camera you have. Are you photographers too?"

"Oh. no." Gloria answered. "My husband teaches at a university, and we take photographs for him to use in his classes."

"What does he teach?" Sophie asked.

William joined the conversation. "I teach architecture. "I study the old cathedrals around the world and incorporate them in my history of architecture classes."

"That sounds very interesting." Sophie replied.

Gloria added, "Every summer we travel to places where there is a cathedral. William photographs them and adds the pictures to his class lectures."

Sophie took their picture with their camera, and they did the same for her. They then started talking about photography. Sophie showed them how to take photographs of the cathedral at different angles to capture the shadows that brought out distinctive features of the design.

"You've been very helpful," Gloria said. "Would you like to join us for lunch? We'd like to treat you since you've been so helpful showing us better ways to capture the designs of the architecture."

Sophie hesitated. She knew she was delaying the inevitable of making a decision to visit the

Ducros family. Besides these people were friendly and she was enjoying talking to them. She accepted the invitation.

Sophie asked them where they traveled to take photos of cathedrals. They said they have been all over Europe starting with the better known cathedrals, then discovered the lesser known ones. William had been teaching for over 25 years, but was not interested in retirement just yet as he enjoyed his work and they loved to travel. Sophie asked if they had children.

"We had a little girl, but she died very young." Gloria said.

"Oh, I'm sorry." Sophie said.

"She had leukemia. She was with us for five years. We were glad to have had her for as long as we did."

Sophie felt as if she were intruding into their private lives so didn't ask anymore about their family. But Gloria started talking about family and asked Sophie about hers. Sophie was feeling more comfortable with the Linkletters, so she told them a little about being adopted and having family in France that she never knew, and was here to find out more about them. She told them that she was hesitant as she didn't know anything about the French side of her heritage, and wasn't sure if these people would want to see her since it might be a reminder of the war.

Gloria got very motherly and told Sophie that she must find her family. "I think they would be overjoyed to see you." Gloria said. "To have a family member show up that they did not know about would seem to me to be a joyous thing. Family is so important. In the end, thats all that matters. Go find them." Gloria said. "Make up for the years that you didn't know each other. You never know how much time you have on this earth, so make the most of it. Spend as much time with your family and friends as you can."

Sophie was surprised at Gloria's encouragement and concern. Gloria explained, "You are about the age that our daughter would be today. When I saw you, the first thing I thought of was her. I don't know why. Perhaps we were meant to meet each other here to give each other support."

William said, "Gloria believes in fate, that things happen the way they are supposed to happen. And everywhere we go and everyone we meet is part of that fate and has some spiritual meaning for all of us."

"That's interesting." said Sophie. "I wonder about that myself sometimes. I wonder if the choices we make are the ones we are supposed to make, or if we could have changed our future by making a different decision at some crucial point in our lives."

"I believe this must be a crucial point in your life then. I think if we had not met, you might have made a decision not to find your family. That's why we met here." Exclaimed Gloria excitedly. "So go now. Go find your family. Go have a wonderful life. I'm so glad we met."

"Thank you, Gloria, but what influence do you think I had on your lives?" Sophie asked.

""It's strange, but the moment I saw you I thought of my daughter. I think she would have been very much like you. That has given me a comfort to think she would have grown up to be someone like you."

"I'm honored that you would think that."

replied Sophie. "Thank you for the lunch and the company. It has been a pleasure."

"Thank you. The pleasure was all ours." said Gloria.

Sophie drove up to the Ducros vineyard. She looked around to see if she could remember any of it. She was told that she was three years old when she was taken from here, and there was a familiarity about the place. She had a vague memory of running around in the fields and being chased by someone. She walked up the steps and knocked on the door. It was opened by an older woman. Sophie asked, "I'd like to see Dominique."

"*Pardon? Je ne parle pas Anglais.*"

"*Qui est-es Rosa?*" said a voice in the background.

"*Oh, pardon moi. Je voudrais parler à' Dominique.*" Sophie said in her best French.

"*Une femme demande à parler à vous, Madame.*" said the woman to the voice in the background.

"Send her in." was the reply.

Sophie was escorted to the library where she saw a woman sitting at a desk. The woman looked up and started to say, "May I help..." but as she was getting up, she froze, staring at Sophie.

Sophie thought, *oh, this is a bad idea, she doesn't look happy.*

Then a huge smile crossed the woman's face as she said, "Sophie? Sophie? Is it really you? What are you doing here?" She came around the desk towards Sophie and opened her arms to give her a hug.

Sophie responded with a hesitant smile as

Dominique kissed her on both cheeks. "I thought I would stop by here to visit you. Cedric said I should come."

"You should have called. Why didn't Cedric call to tell us you were in France?"

"I told him not to call. I wasn't sure if I was coming here or not." said Sophie. "Cedric told me everything after Walter died. I never knew he was my father. I never knew any of this. I wasn't sure what to do. I didn't know if any one here would want to see me."

"Of course we wanted to see you. All those years, we wanted to see you. Cedric informed us all about your life as Walter promised. We are so proud of you. He sent us pictures and kept us up to date on everything you did."

"That's why you recognized me? From the pictures he sent?"

"Yes. I was stunned when I saw you just now. I never thought you would just show up like this. But come, sit down, let's talk. Rosa, bring us some tea." Dominique said. "Tell me everything. Tell me about your life. What are you doing in France?"

"After Cedric told me I was adopted, I didn't know what to do. I was confused, shocked, sad, angry. I went through a lot of emotions. But Cedric told me how everyone loved me. Now I'm just sad that I wasn't given the opportunity to know Walter. Then to find out about my mother's life and death, and your family taking me in after the train was bombed. I'm overwhelmed. I want answers, but I don't even know what questions to ask."

"Yes, we all loved you. After you were taken away, I cried for weeks. I was sad and angry for months. But the war was just over and there was much damage to repair. Then as they say, life goes on, and I eventually realized that you belonged with your father."

"I may have belonged to Walter, but he didn't keep me. He sent me to his cousin to be adopted."

"They loved you and you had a good life with them." Dominique said.

"Everyone keeps telling me that." said Sophie. "I wonder what if he had never found me. I would have grown up here."

"I would have loved that. You were my sister. But before Walter and Theo came here, we didn't know if you were a German baby or not. We didn't know who the women were on that train. The other victims were all German soldiers. Then Walter and Theo showed up and told us that they knew who the women were and we knew then that they would take you away. You must be tired. You will stay the night." It was a statement, not a question. "Come upstairs and I will show you to your room. Rosa will bring your luggage."

"How strange that sounds, 'my room.' Is this where I slept?"

"It was my room too for a long time," said Dominique. "Then my children slept here and my grandchild too. You will meet them at dinner. Come down when you are rested."

Sophie stared out the window of "her" room. She saw the endless fields of grape vines and wondered which ones Dominique chased her in. She saw the road to the house and the train tracks in the distance and thought how it must have looked when the train was bombed. The horror of her mother dying in the wreckage made her shiver. She wondered where the graves were. She would ask

Dominique to show her. Just then a little boy came running up the stairs and into her room disturbing her reverie.

"*Bonne Madame de soirée. Le dîner est prêt.*"

"*Merci, monsieur. Je viens.*" Sophie answered.

Sophie was introduced to Dominique's family at dinner. It was a large family with Dominique's husband, children and the little boy who was her grandson. Dominique's brother and his wife and children were there. Then there was Dominique's father. Etienne Ducros and his wife were the ones who discovered the baby in the wreckage. When Dominique asked him about it, he didn't remember much. Dominique said to Sophie, "He had a stroke a few years ago after our mother died, and doesn't remember anything about the past. He spends most of his time in the wheelchair now. We take him out to the vineyards where he seems to be happy."

Dominique's brother remembered Sophie. "You were such a cute little thing. We loved to watch Dominique play with you and take care of you. Our other brother loved you too, but he was sent to Germany in the work plan and never came back."

"We waited years for him to return. Many boys came back even years later. But he never did. We don't know what happened to him, if he died in the work camps, or stayed in Germany." said Dominique sadly.

"I'm sorry. I can't imagine how it must have been during the war. So many young people having to grow up and fight a war instead of enjoying life. And so many dying young for your country." Sophie said. "But I think that now there is more information coming out about the missing people. Germany is releasing records they kept of the people that were in the camps. Maybe now you can find out what happened to him."

"We would prefer to think that he died there, that he died for our cause rather than staying in Germany. Many of those who came back were never the same. Many people felt that those who went to the German work camps were traitors of some kind. It was such a hard time for everyone. But we must not think of the past. We try to concentrate on now and the future. Our vineyard is doing well and we have our young growing to love the work here." said Dominique.

"It would have been a wonderful place to grow up." mused Sophie. "You would have been a good family to call my own."

"Yes, you are half French. And you seem to remember the language well for being only three when you left."

After dinner, Sophie asked about the graves. "We can visit in the morning." Dominique said.

"I have something to show you." said Sophie. She took out the little book, "*Le Petit Prince.*" "Remember this book that you packed with my things? And look at the photograph you hid inside the cover."

Dominique was brought to tears. "Oh Sophie. Your parents kept the book? I wondered if they had it or if it got lost."

"I found it in my parent's attic. After they died I went through their papers and found it where they kept private documents. Then I saw the photograph sticking out from inside the cover and I wondered who the people were and why my parents had it. Then Cedric told me the story after Walter died."

Dominique's family all passed around the

photograph and marveled at the fact that she had kept it. "I want you to have it." said Sophie.

"Oh, no.! It is for you." Dominique said.

"Cedric made a copy for me. He said you would like to have it back."

"Yes, of course. It is the only photograph taken of us and my brother. Look how young we all were. And those clothes! We look like peasants."

"You were peasants, mother." Dominique's son said laughingly.

Sophie felt so comfortable with the Ducros family. She wished she could spend more time with them. But there were other people she needed to see. In the morning Dominique took her to see her mother's grave.

Sophie looked at the three graves sadly and thought, *this is my mother, and her friend and baby. I don't even know what she looked like. No one has any photographs of her. If she had never been on that train, I might have grown up here in France. I am half French as Dominique said. This is all so strange and confusing. Is this all a dream? Am I that little girl that Dominique played with? Why did people have to keep secrets? What would my life have been like if they all told the truth?*

"I can't imagine what you are feeling." said Dominique. "There are so many graves like this all across our country. You should visit the American Cemetery in Normandy while you are here. We French are so grateful that your countrymen gave their lives for our freedom."

"I will do that. But first I need to go to the village where Walter landed and met my mother. I have to see if there is anyone there that I am related to, or anyone who remembers them. I'd like to find out as much about them as I can."

"You must come back and visit us again. I haven't thought about the war in years. Perhaps that's a good thing. Or perhaps some memories are better left in the dark."

CHAPTER SIXTEEN

Sophie found the vineyard that Cedric said belonged to her mother's family. Cedric told her that Walter found it abandoned when he tried to find Yvette after the war, but it looked to be occupied now. Sophie hesitated to knock, but mustered the courage. A woman answered. Sophie asked her if they knew Henri Legier who lived here during the war. The woman invited Sophie inside and fetched her son who spoke English. Between the son's English and Sophie's French, she found out that the family bought the vineyard many years ago. It had been abandoned for a long time and they didn't know much about its history or the people who lived there before. They told Sophie that the Mayor might be able to give her more information.

The mayor was young and didn't know anything, but he said that his father could probably tell her more. She was welcome to go to his house to talk to him.

The old man said, "*Oui. Je me souviens.* I remember the family. Henri Legier lived there with his two children Yvette and Jean-Paul. Henri's wife died giving birth to Yvette."

Sophie did not tell him that she is Yvette's daughter. She did not want to talk about the war just yet as she knew many older Frenchmen were reluctant to talk about it, so she tried to establish a rapport with him first by talking about how France was a beautiful country and she was enjoying traveling to different cities.

"I suspect you want to talk about the war. Why else would you be here asking about a family that disappeared then?" the old man asked.

So Sophie told him the story about how her father was an American soldier who was shot down nearby and met Yvette who she was told is her mother. She said that Henri would be her grandfather and Jean-Paul would be her uncle, and she was looking for any other family that might be in the area.

The old man nodded and opened up to her about what he knew. "It was so long ago. I haven't thought about the war in years. It was a bad time and many of us want to forget. So many friends and family died or were sent to Germany and never came back. We were devastated. We tried to go on living after the war, but it was so hard."

Sophie did not want to interrupt but was anxious to find out about her family. "Did you know Henri well?"

"Oh yes. We were a small village before the war. Everyone knew everyone else. When the war broke out and the Germans invaded our town, it was such a confusing time. Since I was the Mayor, I had to find a balance between the Vichy government, the Germans, and the local people. After a while, people began to realize that the Vichy government was a pawn for the Germans, but I had to act as if I was supporting it. Many of our young people started to join the Resistance to fight the Germans. I was trying to help them as much as I could while pretending to help the Germans. I knew that Henri was operating a transmitter. The Germans knew someone in the area had one, but couldn't find it. I led them on many different paths to divert them from Henri's vineyard, but eventually they found him. They burned down his barn and took him away. I never saw him again. That happened after Jean-Paul, Henri's son was killed, and Yvette, his daughter had gone to Paris with her friend Hélène. Henri had no other relatives here. His wife died when Yvette was born."

Sophie interrupted again, "So Henri had no other family that you know of?"

"No." the Mayor continued. "But I remember the two American soldiers who were shot down. They stayed for a couple of months, then were rescued. Yvette and Hélène had both gotten pregnant by the soldiers, but they went to Paris and continued to go on clandestine missions. I heard that they were killed in a bombing. So you believe that you are Yvette's child? That is good. Then Henri's legacy will live on."

"What about the other members of the Resistance? Are any of them here?"

"I remember all of the young people from here that were in the Resistance. Of all of them, only Raymond and Cécile came back after the war. Raymond was injured and Cécile took care of him, but they didn't stay here. I guess the memories of their friends haunted them. I heard much about Raymond over the years. He had a talent for music and became a popular singer. I believe they are somewhere in Amiens. He has a tavern there. He would be able to tell you more about the war and his friends."

"Thank you so much for telling me about them. I hope it didn't bring up sad memories for you." Sophie said.

"You are very welcome. Yes, the memories are sad, but we must not dwell on them. We have our freedom thanks to their sacrifices and we must live to make them proud."

Sophie hugged the old man and wished him well.

"Go find Raymond and Cécile. Talk to them about their childhood friends. Go and discover your heritage," he said as they embraced.

Sophie drove back to Amiens to the cathedral where she met the Linkletters. She wandered around looking for the tavern that the mayor told her about. It was a few blocks away near where she had lunch with the Linkletters. They might even have passed it before. Sophie thought about what a coincidence it was that she was right here just a few days ago. The tavern was called *Le Nid de Faucon*. She ordered a café and asked the waiter if he knew of Raymond and Cécile. He told her that they were the owners and lived upstairs, but hardly came into the tavern much anymore. "You might find them in the park," he said. "Madame Cécile often takes him there."

Sophie asked what he meant by that.

"Raymond has been in a wheelchair for the past few years. Cécile takes him everywhere." the waiter said.

At the park, Sophie watched Cécile and Raymond for a while before approaching them. Cécile was talking animatedly to Raymond but he didn't seem to be reacting. He looked lethargic. Sophie walked toward the couple and said to Cécile, "*Pardon moi, Etes-vous Cécile?*"

Cécile answered, "*Oui. Qui êtes-vous? Vous-êtes American?*"

"Mon nom est Sophie. Parlez-vous Anglais?"

"Yes we speak English. Do we know you?" asked Cécile.

"Not exactly." Sophie answered. "But I think you knew someone I am related to. I'd like to ask you some questions. I am searching for people who may have known my parents, and my search has led me to you both."

"Well, I'm curious." said Cécile. "Who is it that led you here? Who is it that we might have known?"

"It's a long story. Is there somewhere that we can go to talk?" Sophie asked.

"There is a private room in the back of *Le Nid de Faucon.* It is just around the corner. Is that alright with you Raymond?" Cécile asked him.

Raymond just shrugged his shoulders as if he didn't care.

As they settled down in the private room, the waiter brought wine, cheese and croissants. Raymond had not said a word yet, but kept looking curiously at Sophie.

"I'd like to get right to the point, if that's ok." said Sophie. "I was told that my father was an American soldier who was shot down near a vineyard. He and his friend were helped by a group of French Resistance fighters. They were rescued a few months later, but became friends with the Resistance while they were here."

"That sounds very familiar, but we don't know of any family related to these soldiers. We helped many soldiers, but knew nothing about the American soldier's children." Cécile said as she look strangely at Sophie. "Tell us more. Who were these people?"

Sophie began the story. "I was adopted, but only found out a few months ago. I never knew until my adoptive parents died. I was contacted by an attorney named Cedric who told me the story about my real parents. He said that my father was an American soldier named Walter, who with his friend Theo was shot down in France. There they met Yvette and Hélène, whose code names were Camellia and Jasmine, and a number of other Resistance fighters, you both included. The soldiers fell in love with the women and both of them had a baby by the soldiers. But by the time the war was over, and they tried to return to France to find the women, they were told that they had all died. Then they were led to a vineyard near where the train was bombed, and the Ducros family told them about the baby that survived. That baby is me. I was three years old when they found me."

Raymond and Cécile both stared at Sophie and exclaimed together, "*Mon Dieu! Est-il possible?*" Then they looked at each other and Raymond said, "*Oui, elle lui ressemble.*" He repeated in English, "I thought there was something familiar about her, but I couldn't place where I would have known her from."

Then Cécile said, "We remember Walter and Theo. They found us after the war. We told them what we knew at the time. We knew that Yvette and Hélène both had an affair with the Americans and both had a baby. We knew that Yvette and Hélène had their babies and were on the train to Amiens when it was bombed. They were coming to meet us to rescue Raymond. We thought that there were no survivors from the train. We told Walter and Theo to go find where they died to pay homage to the women. We thought that Walter and Theo were going to return to America, but must have decided to visit the grave site to see where they were buried. They never came back to tell us what they found."

"Cedric gave me a letter from Walter telling me that I am Yvette's child. I never knew any of this until Cedric contacted me. He was told to give me Walter's letter after Walter died." Sophie said.

"I wish they would have told us." said Cécile. "I would have loved to know that you are Yvette's child."

"For some reason, it was all kept a secret." said Sophie. "Cedric told me that Walter was wounded, and was unable to care for a child. Besides, back then, it was taboo to have a child out of wedlock, so he never told his family either. My adoptive mother was a cousin of his. She could not have children of her own, so they all thought it was the best solution to have her raise me as her own. Even if you were told about me, you would not have been able to contact me."

"But it would have been a reassurance to know that someone survived, and that Yvette's child was saved. They were all our childhood friends. We experienced the best of times together and when the war broke out, we joined the Resistance together. They all died except for us. It was and still is difficult to accept that. Especially Raymond. He and Jean-Paul were the best of friends. He has never gotten over the death of our friends."

"This place, *Le Nid de Faucon,* dosen't that mean Hawk?" Sophie asked.

"Yes, it is The Hawk's Nest. It is named for Jean-Paul. Raymond wrote a song about him. It was very popular for a long time. Raymond, why don't you sing it for Sophie?"

Raymond looked askance at Cécile. "No. I'm tired of remembering. I don't want to be reminded of the war again. I'm tired of the sadness and of the losses."

"I understand that it must be difficult to remember. But I don't know much about my parents. I'm trying to find out who I am. Who was my mother? I don't even have a picture of her. I don't know what she looked like. I only saw Henri's vineyard where she lived, but there were people living there that didn't know who lived there before. Henri was my grandfather, and Jean-Paul was my uncle. I don't know if there was any other family, or anything about them. I would appreciate knowing about them, what you all did before the war, and during the war. I don't wish to upset you, but if it is too hard for you to remember, tell me who else I might be able to talk to, and I will leave you."

"No. Please wait." Cécile begged. " Raymond, it might be good for you to talk about it now. You have this bottled up inside you for too many years. I think you should talk to Sophie about our friends, about the past. She only wants to know about her parents. Anyone should be able to find out about their family history if they can."

"It is because we got involved with that stupid war that I lost my leg, and my friends. The future I envisioned for us was taken away from me. Why should I help her?" asked Raymond.

"You are alive, You were saved. You went on to write and sing beautiful songs. Many people admired you for that. Many people still sing your songs. You don't know what future you would have had if we had not gotten involved with the war. We may have all died anyway." Cécile said.

"Raymond, I might have died on that train." Sophie said. "Why did anyone of us live or die? No one can answer that, but we must go on and live our lives as best we can. If not for ourselves, then for the memory of those that died. They died so that we can live free. They would not want us to give up. I truly believe that if they could tell us anything, they would say to us to make the best of ourselves so that they would not have died in vain."

Raymond stared at Sophie for a long time before he apologized. "You are right, Sophie. I'm sorry. You caught me on a bad day. Will you stay the night and we will talk tomorrow? We have rooms upstairs where you are welcome to stay."

Cécile smiled at Sophie and said, "Come. I'll show you to your room. We can meet here in the morning." As Cécile walked Sophie upstairs, she said, "Thank you for encouraging Raymond. He really needs to talk about the war. He is depressed most of the time lately and I think he feels sorry for himself. Please forgive us He will be better in the morning."

"There's nothing to forgive. I just hope my visit can be helpful to all of us. I didn't mean to cause anyone pain."

Raymond seemed in a better mood at breakfast. He began to talk about his childhood when they were all friends. He remembered everyone, Yvette, her brother Jean-Paul, Hélène, and the others. He told Sophie about how they would play at each other's vineyards and how they knew of all the secret hiding places, and how that helped them hide soldiers and supplies during the war. Then as they got older, the girls went away to school as the boys worked at their families' vineyards learning the business. They didn't pay much attention to what was going on in the world as Hitler was growing in power. It was not until the Germans invaded their land that they became involved in the war. They were young and at first thought that their army would rid their country of the vermin. But it soon became clear to them that their hero from the first world war, General Petain, and others in the government were accepting the invasion and even collaborated with them. General Petain tried to convince the French to accept the German rule. Raymond and the others were soon appalled that their country, the elders and the army, was not fighting back. So the young people began to do simple sabotage incidents, more like childish pranks than anything they thought would rid their country of the Germans. They would cut communication lines, put sugar in the gas tanks, derail trains that carried France's food and other goods across the border to Germany. But they never tried to hurt anyone. Then someone shot and killed a German soldier. The Germans retaliated severely. They began killing Frenchmen, women and children mercilessly. Raymond and his friends were outraged and got serious about taking matters into their own hands. They soon discovered that there were other groups of French people all around the country doing the same things. They heard of the Resistance. They heard on the radio General de Gaulle telling the French people to resist. The Resistance grew and they began to get help from London and the Allies. Lysander planes dropped supplies, money, weapons, food, radios, and men who helped in the use of the weapons and radios and taught them other clandestine activities. That was when the two American soldiers were shot down in the fields near them.

Sophie had heard most of the story from

Cedric and from the letter her father wrote. But Raymond and Cécile's telling of it gave it a personal touch. Here were the people who were there and knew her mother since childhood. She heard of the bravery of her grandfather with his transmitter and how he disappeared. They told her of how Jean-Paul was killed trying to derail a train. That was when most of their other friends were killed. That was when Raymond was wounded and never recovered from that wound.

Cécile told Sophie of Yvette and Hélène's pregnancies. She said that they were able to use the pregnancy and babies to hide documents and befriend the Germans by telling them the babies were from German soldiers. Sophie learned about her mother's bravery in getting information from the Germans and giving that information to the Resistance. Yvette and Hélène were able to get more information than they had hoped for. Sophie thought about how dangerous that was, that they could have been killed if found out, but they did it anyway. They did it for their freedom and their country.

Cécile was telling Sophie about how Yvette and Hélène were on the train to help with the rescue of the Resistance prisoners from Amiens prison when the train was bombed. Sophie was told by the Ducros family that the train was packed with German soldiers. Suddenly she paled as she realized that the train was not bombed by the Germans, but by the Allies. She had to ask.

"Who bombed he train?"

Raymond and Cécile understood the truth at the same time. "Oh, Sophie, Sophie. I'm so sorry. We didn't realize that you didn't know. It was the Allies who bombed the train. They thought it had only

Germans on it. They couldn't have known there were Frenchmen on the train. They couldn't have known Yvette and Hélène and the babies were on that train."

Sophie was stunned. She couldn't speak. She was overwhelmed with horror. "Oh, my God!" she finally blurted out. "It was the Americans who bombed the train and killed my mother.! Oh, my God! I can't....I can't...!" Sophie got up in a daze and left the tavern. She ran and walked and ran trying to absorb what she had just learned. There were people all around her looking curiously at her and she wanted to avoid them. She found herself inside the cathedral where she met the Linkletters. She sat in a pew in the back, tears coming down her face, trying to think, trying not to think.

Eventually she got control of herself and knew she had to return to the tavern. She was passing the park where she first met Raymond and Cécile and saw them there. "I didn't mean to run off like that." she said.

"No need to explain. We were coming to look for you. We understand that the news was a shock. But I think you misunderstood. I said that the Allies bombed the train, but it was not the Americans. I know that probably does not make it any better, but it was a mission organized and led by the Royal New Zeland Air Force. They had planes called Mosquitos that were better at this kind of complicated mission. The planes targeted the walls of the prison so that the people inside could escape. There were 700 *Maquis* and Resistance there, many of them important leaders. They were going to be executed. The mission to rescue them was called Jerico. They targeted the train going to the prison because there were many Germans on it who were going to witness and help with the execution. It was such a hurried decision that there was no time to inform the Allies that there were innocent French women on that train. We weren't even sure that they were on the train. They informed us that they were coming to help because Raymond was in the prison and we were planning a means to hide whoever escaped. Later when we heard the train was bombed and they never showed up, we knew they must have been on the train."

"Couldn't you have gone there to find out?" asked Sophie.

"There was a war going on, Sophie. I escaped but was severely injured. Cécile had to hide me until it was safe to leave the area. We couldn't just go anywhere we wanted." Raymond said bitterly. "Many innocent Frenchmen were unfortunately killed by the Allies. Your country calls that 'collateral damage.' Innocent lives are sacrificed for the greater good and all that. Besides, it could have been worse. It could have been Walter and Theo's mission. They could have been the ones to bomb the train."

"Raymond!" Cécile exclaimed. "How insensitive you are. That was an uncalled for remark. Apologize to Sophie. Stop thinking of yourself for once. Honestly, I don't know why I stay with you."

"I'm sorry Sophie. That was uncalled for. It just makes me sick to think of what wars do to people. It was so senseless. All because of one crazed madman who wanted to rule the world."

"We should go back to the tavern. There is a lot more we can tell you about your mother." said Cécile.

In their private back room of the tavern, Sophie asked Raymond how he got his leg injured.

"I was shot at when Jean-Paul was trying to derail the train. The Germans shot everywhere, not knowing that I was hidden, but a bullet went into my leg. I was supposed to be the look out, but didn't see the Germans. Everyone else was massacred. I made it back to the vineyard. I wanted to continue to help the Resistance to get revenge. I found another group, but because of my injury, could not keep up. On another mission, the others escaped, but I was too slow. That's when I was captured and sent to Amiens prison. There were no doctors and my leg got infected. It wasn't until after the war that I finally got proper medical treatment. By then, it was too late. They tried to save my leg, but with no success. I had part of my leg amputated."

"You are still bitter." Sophie observed. "But I will repeat what I said just yesterday. We have to live our lives the way those who died would have wanted us to live. That is the only way to honor their memory. They died for our freedom and we must make the most of that freedom so their sacrifice would not have been in vain."

Raymond agreed and said he would try not to be negative. He and Cécile talked about their friends and family before the war. Sophie asked about their lives after the war and about Raymond's music. Cécile told her that Raymond became a popular musician and mentioned the song he wrote about Hawk. She said he became famous for a while with that tribute to Jean-Paul. Sophie asked Raymond to sing it for her. At first he objected, but with her and Cécile's encouragement, he agreed. People in the tavern heard the music from the back room and begged Raymond to sing it for them too. Many of the patrons in the tavern knew Raymond and Cécile well.

They encouraged Raymond to sing more songs as he had not done that in a long time.

"Raymond is at home on the stage." Cécile remarked as they sat in the tavern listening to Raymond sing "It is sometimes the only thing that gets him out of his depression. But he doesn't sing much anymore. I try to encourage him to keep singing, but it takes more and more effort to do so. I think your coming here and asking about the past has helped him. He tries to forget and his music takes his mind off of everything. But he needs to realize that our friends who died should be remembered."

"I will never understand wars." said Sophie. "Is it worth the lives of all who gave their lives for what little has been gained?"

"Sometimes much is gained." answered Cécile. "Our country, and all of Europe was freed from a tyrant. All the lives lost should be remembered. All of their sacrifices should be documented. So many members of the Resistance who died have a story to tell but no one to tell it to. You are a journalist, Sophie. Maybe you could tell the stories for them."

"I wouldn't know where to begin. Many people who are still alive are like Raymond and don't want to relive the past."

"You have the skills to encourage them to talk." said Cécile. "Look how you got Raymond to talk about it. You could begin with the story of your own family and our friends. After all, it is your heritage too. Your French family and your American soldier. You should visit the American Cemetery in Normandy. It's very near here. You could go there in the morning and return before dark. We'd like you to stay another day."

"Yes, I'd like that. Dominique also told me to go there. Why don't you both come with me?"

Sophie's heart came up to her throat when she first saw the rows and rows of grave stones lined up like the soldiers they were, at attention waiting for their orders. But there would be no orders for these soldiers anymore. She couldn't speak, She couldn't breathe. Tears blocked her vision and she could hardly see.

"The reality of it doesn't hit you until you see it for yourself." said Cécile.

"All those men, no they were only boys." Sophie choked out the words. "They never had a chance to live to become men and fathers. Most of them so young. All of those lives cut short and for what? For the freedom of others like us? Do we deserve it? Are we living our lives respecting what they died for?"

"As they say, did we learn from history?" Cécile replied. "I would think not. We continue as a human race to kill each other. We continue to fight over what? Ideas? Ideals? Religion? Land? Sometimes I think we don't even know what we are fighting for. We follow our leaders blindly trusting that they know what they are doing. That's what the German soldiers did. A few realized that their leader was insanely slaughtering innocent people, but most did what they were told without question."

"And if I write about this and document it with photos, will it make a difference? Will people read and understand that we can't continue to do this? Will it matter?" asked Sophie.

"Maybe, maybe not. But you have to try. You have to do what you believe in. If it matters or not to other people, it must matter to you."

"That sounds like the meaning of life." Sophie half joked.

"It might be just that. The meaning of life is whatever it means to you and you alone." said Cécile.

"What was the meaning for all these soldiers who died so young? Most of them believed in fighting for the freedom of a country they knew little about and for people they didn't know."

Raymond spoke up, "Most of them were young and idealistic, just like we were then. We thought we could drive out the evil that infected our country and we did. But there is so much evil in the world. One evil replaces another. People still hurt and kill each other in groups or as individuals. We keep trying to rid the world of evil, but evil keeps popping up everywhere. It is tiring and sometimes seems like a losing battle."

"That doesn't mean we should stop trying." said Cécile.

"Yes, you are right." Raymond replied. "But one person can't change the world."

"One person did change the world." said Sophie. "Hitler, for example. What if he had never been born? Do you think someone else would have done what he did?"

"There have been many conquerors throughout history, and there will be many more. We have to believe that the good people will not stop fighting them. I don't think we will ever rid the world entirely of evil. Having a utopian world seems like an impossible dream." Cécile said.

"That's because there are fanatical people who have enough charisma to convince others to follow them. What I don't understand is how so many people can't think for themselves and that they actually believe in the crazy fanatic's ideas." said Sophie.

"So many good people die while so many evil ones live." said Raymond. "Where's the balance in that?"

"Sophie, you could make a difference, even if it is a small one. Who knows how many people you have already influenced by your stories. You have a name that many people already know and would read something that you wrote. If you took some time to travel around France and see all the memorials to the brave soldiers who gave their lives for a cause and of the ordinary French people who helped, like your mother and our friends, and document the stories, maybe some people will think about the damage that wars cause and change their way of thinking about it."

"I would like to do that." answered Sophie. "Besides this memorial to the American soldiers, are there any memorials to the Resistance fighters?"

"There are memorials all over France, especially where the Resistance made a big impact on the outcome of the war, and in the hometowns of those who died. You could start where we fought and Jean-Paul and our friends died. That would add a personal side to your story. There is a small marker there." Cécile said as she looked at Raymond. "I think it would do Raymond good to see it again."

Sophie read the marker where her uncle, Jean-Paul died. She thought of her mother's grave and of all their friends who were part of the Resistance groups in France who gave their lives for their country. She decided then that she must write their stories. She drove Cécile and Raymond back to the tavern and told them good-by. She called Cedric and told him of her plans and thanked him. Then she traveled throughout France finding places where there were monuments, markers and people who remembered the war and were willing to talk to her. After months of visiting most of the memorials, she decided that she had enough information to write their stories. She returned to New Orleans to work on her book.

PART FIVE

CHAPTER SEVENTEEN

Sophie met with Tessa at their favorite meeting place, Brennan's Restaurant, for brunch. There they caught up with each other's lives. Tessa told Sophie what she has been doing for the past year.

"I had been working at the battered women's clinic for years as they were opening up new clinics around the state. Eventually I became a manager going to the new clinics to help them set up. By then I was earning enough money to quit teaching. This new job is so much more fulfilling, besides it's something that I enjoy doing. I have first hand knowledge about what these women are going through and what they need to change their lives by getting away from their abusive husbands. It was shocking to find out how many women are living with abuse when years ago I thought I was the only one. I had no idea it was such a widespread problem. So many abusive men. How and why is this happening? I want to help find some answers. We need more clinics all over the country."

"How do you get the funding?" asked Sophie.

"Most of it comes from donations, and we get some government help. As the problem becomes more recognized, the funding has increased. So much more is needed though. We are working on campaigns and TV commercials to raise awareness to the problem."

"I can see that you are more excited about this job than you were when you were teaching."

"It is not so much that I enjoy this work, but it is knowing that I am making a difference in so many lives. They are getting an opportunity that I never had. I had no one to turn to, but these women now have somewhere to go to where they see that there is a way out for them and they can make a better decision about their future."

"What do you do about the husbands? Especially the ones who won't let go? The ones who try to keep their wives from leaving even by threatening them?"

"That's where our safe houses over the state and country help. Very few people know where these houses are except the social workers and medical personnel who refer these women to us. We have established a network of underground movements where the women that we think are in danger can get away. It is especially complicated if there are children involved. Sometimes it is necessary to give them a new identity. With some of the funding, we can move women to a new location with a new name. We establish them with some funds until they can get jobs."

"Do the husbands ever find them?" asked Sophie.

"Very seldom. Most of the men eventually give up or find another target and remarry. We try to offer those men help by referring them to social workers, but few of them take that opportunity. The biggest problem with them is that they don't think they did anything wrong. Sometimes the women return when they think the danger has passed and their exes are no longer interested in them. Then they can start a new relationship with a better understanding of how they got in the trap of abuse in the first place."

"It is because you went through that terrible experience that you are able to help establish what is needed now?"

"I believe so. The women can relate to me when I tell them of my past. Then they open up to me. I wish we could do more. There are so many women in this situation that our safe houses are filling up too fast. Part of what we need to do is understand why the abusers are that way and what can we do to change that. It is a problem for the entire society. We need funding to start programs in the schools to teach children what is acceptable behaviors. I know when I was in the classroom I saw so much about dysfunctional families that needs to change. But there was nothing I could do then."

"Yes, society has changed. Remember when we were in school, we never thought of having a career of our own? We thought our destiny was to be someone's wife and mother. We thought we had to be identified by who we married."

"You have done things that have helped change women's ideas." said Tessa.

"Do you think so?" replied Sophie.

"Yes. You broke out of the mold. You chose a career over marriage. You showed many women that they don't have to settle for married life if they have a dream to do something else, then regretting what they might have done if they got married instead."

"But remember, I was offered that job because of my father's interference. Would I have been able to get that kind of opportunity if he hadn't arranged for me to go with Doris and Len? Would I have married

Wayne instead and been one of those women who always wondered what it would have been like to have a career as a Journalist? Would I have had children and forgotten about my dream?"

"But you didn't. You were comfortable enough with yourself that you chose to go out and follow your dream and leave Wayne behind. You didn't give in to the pressure of needing to get married to have an identity. That's what I thought for myself back then. Anyway, I didn't have any other dream or career that I wanted."

"I'm not sure that's what I was thinking then. I just had the opportunity to do this one thing before getting married and I did it. Then the opportunities kept coming. When I found out that it was my father who manipulated the opportunities, I felt that my life was not my own."

"It was still your choice. You could have quit at any time and married Wayne instead."

"That's what people keep telling me, and I guess you're right. I loved what I was doing. I couldn't stop especially when I was told that I was good at it and got awards for my work. I was so involved with my career that I never looked back."

"I suppose the problem with young women just out of high school or even college is that they don't really know what to do with their lives, so they get married. Then their lives are bound up with their family and they forget about any dream they had of a career."

"Is that what you think you did?" asked Sophie. "You got married because you didn't know what else to do with your life?"

"I'm sure that's what I did." answered Tessa. "I didn't have any idea of what else to do. Besides I thought that if I didn't marry Geoff, I probably would not meet anyone after graduation. If I had waited to get to know his family better maybe I would not have married him. I might have seen his family for what it was."

"You don't know that. I've played the 'What If' game many times. It doesn't help spending time wondering what might have been. I've learned that you have to take each day as a new beginning and start fresh from there."

"I know you are right. I had to learn the hard way. Remember that song *I Did it My Way?* I used to think that I didn't do anything my way and regretted much of my life, but after I got involved in this new job and found a new direction, I realized one day that I stopped feeling that way. Now I get up each morning anxious to go to work, grateful for what I have and what I am doing and go forward from there."

"This may not be the future that we had in mind, and we certainly changed from the innocent naive kids that we were, but we are both doing something of our own choice now. We are both doing something that may help other people. You're helping women who are in an abusive relationship and my stories are helping people understand the impact that wars have on society. It's not just the soldiers who died, but the families and friends they left behind. And those that survived the war, those soldiers and their families are also affected. Maybe there was some guiding hand that we had no control of shaping our lives, but now we control our own future. It makes me wonder if there is such a thing as fate."

CHAPTER EIGHTEEN

When Sophie got home, there was a letter from the publishing company that she sent her manuscript and documentary to. She was surprised to hear from them so soon as it was only a couple of months that she submitted the information. The company wanted more information from her and requested a meeting. The company headquarters was in Chicago. She made arrangements to go there.

She found the building along South Michigan Avenue. She looked up at the skyscraper as the wind blew gusts of dust and debris around her. She wrapped her coat closer around her and took a deep breath. *Why am I so nervous?* She wondered. *It's not like I haven't had my works published before. Maybe because this is is so personal and more important than anything I have done before.*

In the lobby she found the company on the directory. Griffin Publishing Company headquarters, 35th floor. As she stepped out of the elevator, she was taken aback by the beautiful view out the floor to ceiling window overlooking Lake Michigan. The secretary laughed and said, "We get that reaction all the time. It's a gorgeous view isn't it?"

"Yes. It's absolutely breathtaking. How do you get any work done? I'd be staring out the window all day."

"Believe it or not, we get used to it."

"Miss St. Pierre? How pleased I am to meet you." said a voice from behind her.

"This is our CEO, Mr......."

"Just call me Ted." He interrupted the secretary. "Please come into my office."

"I'm very glad to meet you, Ted. You can call me Sophie."

"Actually we've met before, but you probably don't remember."

"I think I would remember meeting someone like you." Sophie blushed as she looked into his pale blue eyes embarrassed by her confession.

"It was a long time ago. You were at a convention of publishers where you received an award for your children's book. I was quite impressed as you were so young to have received such an honor bestowed on you."

"Thank you, but I had great teachers. I learned from the best and had plenty of help. It wasn't completely my own doing." Sophie said not wanting to tell him that she thought she probably got that award because of her father's influence.

"Nevertheless, it was a remarkable achievement."

"How is it that I don't remember you?" she asked out loud but mainly to herself.

"I was very young too. I was there with my father who started this company. I was just learning the business and was there to meet with the other big name publishing companies. But let's get down to business, shall we?"

"Certainly. I brought my manuscript of the book, and the film that I took for the documentary, as you requested."

"First. Let's discuss the book. It is very well

written and would be a great addition to any library. However I don't think it will be on any best seller list."

Sophie felt disappointed, "Why would you think that?"

"Because it is about World War II. The general public does not buy history books. They're more interested in novels. And the people who are old enough to have lived then are tired of reading about that war. It was so long ago for them that they don't want to think of it anymore. They prefer to forget it. Younger people don't want to read about a war that was before their time. They experienced the Viet Nam war that was not very popular, as you probably know. Having said that, I think your book would do well in college and university libraries, and public libraries as well, but not so much in book stores. It doesn't mean we won't consider publishing it. I just mean it will not be a major money maker."

"I'm not really interested in making lots of money. I thought it was a great story about another side of the war that most people don't realize and I wanted to document it before those involved all died, and there would be no one to remember them."

"You are right, it is an interesting read, but mostly I'm interested in your documentary."

"I thought you were a book publisher. Why would you be interested in a documentary?"

"After my father retired and I took over the company, I started a division that produces films. Not the Hollywood type films. Since the advancements in television with people signing up for cable companies with multiple channels, there has been a significant increase in sales of documentaries to independent start up channels.

Viewership of these channels has increased substantially in the past few years. People seem to like the variety to choose to watch shows other than your basic sitcoms and detective stories. I did my research and decided to get in on the ground floor of this new technology age. My company produces more documentaries than you realize."

"I see. So you think my documentary would be good for television?"

"Yes. And it would reference the book. So the documentary would publicize the book and visa versa."

"So each would increase the sale of the other? I see why your father trusted you to take over the business. You have some clever and forward thinking ideas."

"He was old school. But he was smart enough to realize that new blood and new ideas have to come from and for this new generation of technologically savvy people. Enough about that. Did you bring the film?"

"Yes. I have it on tapes from my video camera."

"I have a set up in the next room to view the tapes. Would you have time to stay a while and show some of them to me?"

Sophie and Ted spent the entire afternoon watching and discussing her videos not realizing how late it was until the secretary knocked on the door. "I'm sorry to interrupt, but it's late and I was wondering if you need me anymore."

"Oh, I didn't realize how late it is." Ted replied. "Go on home. I'll close up. Sophie, I'm sorry I kept you so late. Do you have plans for the evening? I'd like to treat you to dinner since I took up your whole day."

"I don't really have any plans. I was just going back to the hotel, maybe do a little sightseeing and find a place to eat."

"Well then, it's settled. You must let me take you to dinner. What kind of food do you like?"

"I like all kinds of food. I don't really have a favorite."

"Then you accept. I know just the place."

The Pump Room was crowded even for a Thursday night, but Ted had no trouble getting a table. "I think you will like this place. There are lots of interesting choices on the menu."

"How did you get a table so fast?" Sophie wanted to know.

"I come here often enough that I have a standing reservation."

"You mean you have celebrity status? You must be well known here. Tell me about yourself."

"I'd rather hear about you. I know a little about you, but nothing personal. For instance, why is such a beautiful woman like you not married?"

Sophie didn't want to reveal too much personal information. She thought Ted was handsome and smart, but a little overly assertive, too sure of himself. She gave him a short answer. "I almost got married out of college, but chose a career instead. I have been on lots of dates, but no one seemed important enough for me to give up my career for." She then diverted the conversation to himself. "What about you? Are you married?"

"I'm divorced. It was friendly. We have two wonderful children that I see a lot of. They live in the suburbs near here."

After dinner, Ted took Sophie back to her hotel. She was glad that he didn't ask to come up to her room as she was not interested in him romantically. She liked him. He was clever and easy to talk to, but she didn't want to get involved too quickly, if at all. She would meet him again Friday morning at his office to continue their discussion of her works.

"Your video is very well done, but the voice over is rather crude." he told her after looking at more tapes. "I can edit that out. I have many celebrities that I can contact that do dialogue on our documentaries."

"I assumed that would have to be done. I was just talking about where I was, what I saw, and taping some of the conversations I had with the older people that were in the war and were willing to talk to me."

"My father was in France during the war. He would be interested in seeing your work. I happen to be going there this weekend. Would you like to come with me and meet him? He might have some information to add to your stories."

At first Sophie hesitated, not wanting to intrude on his family, but he assured her that would not be a problem. "It's a big house with a guest house on the property. You wouldn't be any trouble at all."

Ted picked her up at the hotel early Saturday morning. It was a beautiful drive north along Lake Michigan up to his parents home in Lake Bluff. As they entered the security gates, Sophie gasped when she saw the beautiful estate ahead. At the end of a long driveway between exquisitely sculpted gardens, was an immense colonial three story house. "Don't be intimated." Ted said when he saw her reaction. "We are really regular people. My father's success in the publishing business has given us the opportunity to live extravagantly, but we support many charities."

"Do you live here?" Sophie asked.

"Not since I got married and then took over the company. I have an apartment in town, but I spend some weekends and summers here with my kids so they have time with their grandparents."

"I hope you told them you were coming with a guest." Sophie said warily.

"Of course, I called my mother last night. She'll be delighted to meet you. She loves company. My father goes hunting a lot and she gets bored."

Ted's mother was charming as he introduced her to Sophie.

"Ted, show Sophie to the guest house. That is unless you two have a different plan."

"No mother. We're not sleeping together. Just because I have a lady friend doesn't mean we're having an intimate relationship." And to Sophie he said. "I'm sorry for my mother's comment. She's trying to be a modern woman."

"I am a modern woman. I have to keep up with the times." She said. "You have to stay contemporary if you want to survive in today's world."

Sophie laughed inwardly as she remembered her experience at Woodstock and how she got unexpectedly high. She thought her mother would have been horrified if she knew. "I suppose you are right. The world is changing so fast that we sometimes have to change our beliefs just to keep up."

"I like you already." Ted's mother said to her. "Why don't you show Sophie around after you take her to the guest house. Dinner will be ready at 6. Your father should be home by then."

Ted took Sophie on a tour of the house and grounds while he talked about his children and family. Sophie talked a bit about growing up in New Orleans, and the places she had gone to for her journalism career, but did not want to confide in him about her being adopted. She didn't explain why her interest in France during World War II was a personal decision. Nor had she shown him the photos and videos of the Ducros family or Cecile and Raymond and her visit to Amiens.

Sophie changed and went to the main house for dinner. Ted and his mother were just sitting down while the servants brought out the food. Ted got up as his father entered the dinning room and was starting to introduce him to Sophie. When Sophie rose to shake his hand, he stopped in his tracks. He looked at Sophie as if he had seen a ghost. "What's going on here?" he choked out the words. He grabbed his chest and started breathing heavily. The family thought he was having a heart attack. Ted and his mother went to his side asking him what's wrong. "Call 911! What's happening? Calm down! Sit! Breath!" Everyone was shouting.

Ted's father kept staring at Sophie. She didn't know how to react. Did she do something wrong? Why was he staring at her like that? Had she done something to him that she doesn't remember? She thought she recognized him from the banquet years ago that Ted mentioned. She knew he was the CEO of Griffin Publishing Company. But she had no contact with him other than at the banquet. So why is he still staring at her?

Dinner was forgotten as the emergency

personnel arrived and attended to him. He kept insisting that he was ok and didn't need to go to the hospital. The EMT's got his pressure down to normal, but could not transport him to the hospital if he didn't want to go. Finally he practically threw them out as he claimed to be recovered and that it was not a heart attack. When the EMT's were sure he was stabilized, they left giving the family instructions to watch him and call them back if he showed signs of stress and to call his physician.

He did not want to go to bed as everyone wanted him to do. Instead he insisted that he wanted to go into his library. No one wanted him to be alone, but he said there is a phone and intercom and he will call out if he needs anything. Everyone sat around in a nearby room listening for any signs of distress. Finally after an hour had passed, he called to Ted to accompany him. Ted sat down and his father got right to the subject. "Why did you bring her here?"

Ted was startled to think that Sophie was the cause of his father's troubling reaction. He asked his father, "Why? What's wrong with her? Did she do something to you?"

"No. She didn't do anything to me. How do you know her. Are you having an affair?"

Again, Ted was shocked by his father's bluntness. And he seemed angry which was puzzling since he said Sophie didn't do anything to him. But he had to ask his father, "No. I'm not having an affair with her. Are you?"

"No!" His father answered. "I need to know how you are involved with her, and why did you bring her here."

"You never were that interested in my personal

life before, so why now? Who is she that you are so upset with her being here? I only just met her this week. She didn't say anything about knowing you. She sent a proposal for a book and documentary about France's involvement in World War II. I thought it was interesting so I asked her to meet with me. I have heard of her before and I knew her work was good. I knew that you were in World War II also, so I asked her to come here to meet with you. I think you need to tell me what this is all about."

His father seemed to calm down after Ted's explanation. He stared out the window for a long time until Ted thought he had forgotten he was there. He turned slowly back to Ted and said, "I guess it's about time to explain. I never thought it would come to this, but I think she needs to know the truth. Then you will understand why I reacted like I did. Go get Sophie. Tell her I'd like to apologize for upsetting dinner and her visit here."

"Know the truth about what? What are you talking about?" Ted asked annoyed that his father was being so mysterious.

"Just go get her and I'll talk to both of you."

Ted knocked on the door to the guest house. "I'm sorry to disturb you. I hope you weren't sleeping. My father wants to see you to apologize for his reaction."

"I couldn't sleep." Sophie said. She was confused and upset over Ted's father's reaction to her. "I hope I didn't do anything wrong. I don't know why he kept staring at me like that. I feel it's my fault for upsetting him, but I don't know what I did. Am I intruding on your family? Maybe you should just take me to the train station and I'll go back to the hotel."

"No. It'll be fine. He is feeling much better now. He's calm. But he wants to apologize to you."

"Oh, that's not necessary. He doesn't have anything to apologize for."

"I have no idea what's going on, but he wants to explain something to you. Please come back to the house and see him. I'd like to know what's happening too."

Ted's mother was just leaving the library when Ted and Sophie arrived. His mother seemed concerned but not angry. She told them that his father was feeling better and that he wanted to see Sophie and Ted to discuss what they were working on. "He told me not to worry, that he is fine. He said he really wants to see Sophie's work. I don't understand, but if that's what he wants to do, well, he always did things his own way. He told me to go to bed as I would be bored listening to you all. Please don't let him get overexerted. Make him go to bed if he gets tired." She kissed Ted goodnight.

"Don't worry, mom. I'll be sure and see that this doesn't take long."

"Sit, Sophie, please." Ted's father said. "I've thought about this day for a long time. I was taken aback when I saw you here, Sophie, but knew that someday this might happen. I should have done this a long time ago, but kept thinking it could wait another day, then another day, until the days turned out to be years."

Sophie and Ted looked at each other to see if either of them knew what he was talking about. They both shrugged their shoulders and turned back to his father.

"Dad?" Ted said. "What's going on here?"

"Let me explain." His father said. "First I'd like

to apologize to you Sophie. I didn't mean to react the way I did. I was completely surprised when I saw you here."

"Do you know Sophie?" Ted asked again.

"I told you that I haven't met her, but I do know about her. Now if you will stop interrupting me, I'd like to tell this my way."

"As you know, Ted, I was a pilot in World War II. I never spoke much about it. There were a lot of things that happened there that I wanted to forget, but many things that I could not ignore. There are secrets that only a few other people know about and most of them are dead. Sophie, you know them all."

Sophie looked curiously at Ted's father. The only secret she knew is her adoption and her biological father who was also a pilot. Then it dawned on her. "You are Theo. You are Walter and Cedric's friend. Yes. And Griffin was your code name that is the name of your publishing company. I should have guessed."

"Yes, Sophie. I am Theo. I was with your father in the war and I know all about the circumstances of your adoption."

"You are adopted?" said Ted. "You never told me that."

"I just met you. I don't discuss my private life with strangers." and to Theo she said, "Then you also knew my mother and all of the other Resistance people that I met in France?"

"Yes. I knew them all. And I know what Cedric has told you and about your visit to France meeting with all the people we knew then; your family, the Legier's, the Ducros family who found you and kept you, Cécile and Raymond, all of them."

"Then you can tell me all about your time in

France and things the others may not remember?"

"Well, this ought to be interesting, since you never told us much about that time. But that doesn't explain your reaction to Sophie at dinner. Why should that have upset you?" interrupted Ted.

"I told you not to interrupt. I have to tell the story my way, and your interruptions distract me. Before I continue, I have to ask you, Ted, that you will not tell your mother any of this."

"Why? What is it you don't want her to know?" asked Ted.

"There are many things that happen in a war. Many things that we choose not to talk about. You will find out when I finish my story. But if you feel that you cannot keep some secrets, then I will have to ask you to leave. However there are things you should know since you have befriended Sophie and I don't want things to get out of hand."

"Now I am really curious. So, ok, I agree."

Sophie was getting more curious too. "All I want to know is what you can tell me about my parents. I have so many questions. I was upset that all of you who knew that I was adopted chose to keep it a secret. I was denied the opportunity to know my real father, and now that you were there and obviously kept in touch with Cedric, I want to know why you also chose not to contact me, especially if Cedric told you that I was interested in finding out about Walter and Yvette."

"I understand that you were upset, but remember that those were hard times, different times. Society back then was not as accepting as it is today. But once we shared this secret, and we got on with our lives, it became harder and harder to reveal it. Besides you had the best of everything. Your adoptive parents could not have loved you more."

"Yes, I heard that from Cedric and the letters he gave me from them and Walter. I have accepted that. All I want now is to know about my heritage."

"Then let me continue. Pardon me if I repeat things you already know, but I want Ted to hear the whole story. Sophie, your father, Walter, was my friend and buddy in the war. We were pilots and flew together on missions in France. He and I came to America from Britain when we were young. Our fathers were brothers and printers who wanted to open a company here. We were cousins."

"You never told me you were cousins. I thought you were bitter enemies. You were both CEO's of major publishing companies and gave the world the impression that you hated each other."

"Yes, we laughed about that. It was good for business. The media picked up on a misunderstanding we had and blew it all out of proportion. It drew attention to us and our sales rose, so we encouraged the image of our rivalry and joked about it in private. It was the best advertisement we could have had. We remained good friends though and kept in touch, especially since we were concerned about Sophie's welfare. But let me get back to my story."

Theo began by telling them about how they became pilots. He said that when they were young they learned to fly. "We were so reckless, I'm surprised that we didn't crash our planes, but we loved flying. We decided that we wanted to become pilots for an airline. By the time we were old enough to apply, the war broke out. We had become American citizens by then. When our parents told us that Hitler was bombing Britian and our families had relatives there, we wanted to join the Air Force. We weren't accepted, I don't remember why. But we heard that companies in Canada were taking on pilots who were rejected. So we went to Canada, then to London. Early on and without much more training, we were soon sent on bombing runs. Although it was a war we were having the time of our lives. We loved the danger and excitement. It was an exhilarating experience. We were sent on many missions all over, then France became our target. Once our mission leader found out about the Resistance groups needing supplies, we were sent there. Instead of bombs, we dropped supplies and parachuted men to different locations. Sometimes we landed in fields to pick up men and information. Even though we weren't dropping bombs, we still thought it was exciting because we were dodging the German planes that were trying to shoot us down. One day, they succeeded. We were in a Lysander plane together. Those kind of planes were easy to land in the small fields. The Germans spotted us and we were shot down. Our plane was hit, but we were able to drop supplies and parachute out before the plane crashed. The Resistance group that we were to land near found us and most of the supplies that we dropped. They hid us out and the Germans never found us."

"That's where you and Walter met my mother." Sophie asked.

"Yes, and the other members of the Resistance they worked with. You met with Cécile and Raymond. I'm sure they told you about our time there."

"They did, but Raymond was reluctant to talk about it. He was depressed, but Cécile encouraged him to tell me what happened."

"When London got news of our survival, they were going to send a rescue plane for us. We would have to stay there for a month as they only sent out missions during the full moon. We didn't want to sit around that long so we started helping the Resistance. Henri Legier, Yvette and Jean-Paul's father, had a vineyard with many old unused buildings that we hid in. Some of his neighbors had evacuated to southern France early on so there were many unused buildings we could hide in. Jean-Paul was a leader of sorts as his group of Resistance followed his lead. His sister, Yvette and her friend Hélène took us with them on some of their missions. We didn't know their names at first because they all had code names. If anyone was captured, they would not be able to give the Gestapo much information, they would only know the code names so the Germans would have a hard time finding anyone. Even we had code names. Walter was Dragon and I was Griffin. The girls, Yvette was Camellia and Hélène was Jasmine."

"Yes. Raymond told me that. Jean-Paul's code name was Hawk, Raymond was Raven, and Cécile was Lilac. Raymond wrote a song about Hawk and he sang it for me. He became a well known singer in France." Sophie said.

"I knew a little of that." said Theo. "Cedric kept us informed about him, and we followed his career."

"Why didn't you ever go visit them?" Sophie asked. "I think he and Cécile would have appreciated that. Raymond was always depressed. You might have cheered him up, especially if he knew that I, Yvette's daughter, survived."

"We discussed that, Walter, Cedric and I. We were going to go, but the first few years after we found you, it was too painful to return, then things happened, life happened, and plans got changed. We branched off from our father's printing company and started our own companies, married and started families. We thought to just let things be. So we never went back. We didn't forget them though. We helped Raymond and Cécile get their café."

"He didn't tell me that."

"Raymond didn't know. We loaned him the money for very little interest through a company we established just to help him."

"What company is that?" asked Ted.

"You would never find it." Said Theo. "It's a company within a company within a company. It was abolished after we gave Raymond and Cécile all the help we could."

"Why did everything have to be so secretive?" asked Sophie. "If you had all told the truth long ago, none of this would be happening."

"None of what? You, Sophie are the only one affected by our secret. No one was hurt. You were loved. You had everything you needed."

"No one was hurt?" Ted exclaimed. "How can you say that? We are all affected. You and Walter lied to your families. Your whole life was a lie."

"Since when are you so sanctimonious? You cheated on your wife and are divorced because of it. Who knows if you might not have a child you don't know about with the women you slept with?"

Sophie intervened. "Stop. You are both being childish. We don't know how our lives would have been different if you and Walter told the truth long ago. So the point is moot. You can't change what happened. We just need to figure out what to do now. Where do we go from here. I want to hear the rest of the story. I want to know more about my parents."

Ted and Theo agreed. Theo continued the story. "We were not rescued the next month because the weather was bad and the plane did not come. By then Walter and I spent so much time with Yvette and Hélène and the others that it changed our lives. We saw how they were willing to sacrifice their lives for their country and their beliefs. They did things that were so dangerous, that our stunts as pilots were nothing compared to what the Resistance were doing. We were sometimes face to face with the Germans and were scared, but the Resistance stood up to them. Their bravery was awe-inspiring. Our recklessness was for fun, but they risked everything for something we could never have understood unless we were there. Our emotions were high. While we were in Paris we heard bombings and gunfire. We saw people, innocent people shot, executed, even women and children. It was an unbelievable experience. It was a war, but it didn't make any sense. Why were the Germans killing innocent people? Warfare was not supposed to be like that. Even wars had rules, but the Nazi's didn't care. They didn't follow any rules. They murdered and raped the whole of France. We couldn't let them win. We couldn't let that kind of people rule Europe. What kind of world would we be living in if they had won?"

"Dad. I think you are rambling."

"No. I'm reminiscing. I never talked much about the war before. It feels good to be able to explain how it was. Spending time with those remarkable people was a turning point in our lives. The more time we spent with them, the more we changed. We experienced things that no one, especially all those young people, should have to go through. They risked their lives for their beliefs without giving it a second thought. They did daring and unbelievable things to rid their country of the Nazis. The price of their freedom was high, but they were willing to pay it. We admired and respected them, and yes, we fell in love with them. Walter and Camellia, myself and Jasmine. It was a time when we thought we might not live another day. Any day could have been our last. Those feelings led to a special kind of closeness and we felt we had to live our lives to the fullest. So we lived and loved each day grateful that we were still alive. Then the worst happened. Jean-Paul and the others went to take out a train filled with Jews that was on the way to the German concentration camps. The Germans had spies everywhere and found out about it. The Resistance were ambushed and they were all shot and killed. The girls and Walter and I didn't go on that mission. Raymond survived because he was the lookout and the Germans didn't see him. He was shot in the leg with a stray bullet and found his way back to Henri's vineyard. It was devastating. They were our friends, but worse for Yvette, Hélène and Cécile. They were childhood friends and Jean-Paul was Yvette's brother and Henri's son. We had cheated death many times but had never seen it up close like that. We lost good friends and France lost too many remarkable young people. That was when we lost our cockiness and arrogance. We understood then that there was more to life than our self satisfaction. We were never the same after that."

"You were in love with Jasmine?" Ted asked. "Did you ever tell mother about it?"

"No. And I asked you to keep it a secret. If I

want to tell her, I will on my own time."

"Go on." said Sophie. "Please, finish the story."

"It was a couple of months before London was able to send a rescue plane for us. By then we didn't want to leave, but orders were orders and we had no choice. We vowed our love for Camellia and Jasmine and told them we would return when we could, that the war could not last forever. It was just before we got on the plane that they told us their real names. Camellia and Jasmine were Yvette and Hélène. We told them we would return to France to live with them or take them to America. It didn't matter, we just wanted to be with them. We gave them our address in New Jersey and told them to write to us if they could. There was no way to contact them during the war as the only communication allowed was for important messages concerning the war. Even through Henri's transmitter, we tried sending them a message when we could. We don't know if he ever got our messages. We could write, but we knew that the Germans monitored everything, so if we sent letters we didn't know if they would get to them. Anyway we were so caught up in our missions that we didn't have time for much else. Then we went on bombing missions in Germany. We were shot down again and were able to parachute out before the plane crashed, but this time we were captured. We were sent to one of the German prison camps. I was slightly wounded, but Walter had more serious injuries. He incurred shrapnel on the left side of his body from being shot at. His leg could have been saved but the prison camp didn't have proper medical care, so his wounds festered. We spent a few months in the camp when we heard that the Allies landed in Normandy. We thought the war was finally over, but it took months before we were rescued from the prison camp. Walter was in really bad shape. I didn't think he would make it. I think if we had spent another week there, he would have died."

"Walter didn't write much about being in the prison camp." said Sophie. "I didn't know he almost died there."

"That was a time we didn't want to remember. The only thing that kept us going was thinking about Yvette and Hélène and getting back to them." Theo continued. "After we were rescued from the German prison camp, we were taken to a hospital in London, but there were so many wounded soldiers it was still difficult to get treated. When we finally got sent home, Walter was still in bad shape. He had to have his leg amputated. His wounds were that severe on his left side. He was told that he probably would not be able to have children. After we were discharged, we returned home. Our parents visited us when we were in the hospital, but didn't give us our belongings from the war, thinking that it was too much of a reminder of the war. Finally we were released from the hospital and went home. When we were able to go through our things and the letters that were sent to us, we found the letters from Yvette and Hélène. There were only a couple but the last one told us that they were each pregnant. There were no more letters. So much time had passed, it was over three years, that we figured they must have had the babies. We then made arrangements to go to France and find them. We first went to the vineyard where we met them, but no one was there. The neighbors told us where we could find Raymond and Cécile. That's when we were told that Yvette and Hélène were on a train that was bombed. We were devastated and were going to return home, but Cécile said we ought to go to the village to visit their graves and pay our respects. That's when we found that you had survived. We talked to the Ducros family and the other people of the village to see what they could tell us about the survivors, if they knew whose baby had survived. We were told that the bodies of Yvette and Hélène were so badly burned that they could not describe the women."

"What?" Ted and Sophie both realized what Theo had just implied.

"Wait! Are you saying that you don't know for sure that Sophie is Yvette's child? That she could be Hélène's child? Oh, man! That means that if Sophie is your child by Hélène, then she is my half sister!" said Ted. "That's why you were so upset when you saw Sophie. You thought that if she is your child and we were having a relationship, then, Oh my God!"

"Oh my God." exclaimed Sophie as she looked from Theo to Ted. "Walter might not be my father? *You* might be my father?"

"Yes, Sophie. We didn't know whose child you were."

"But Walter's letter said I was his child. All those years he kept track of me and visited when I graduated."

"We both did. I was there too."

"Walter never said that in his letters, nor did my parents."

"I wanted Walter to believe that you were his child. He couldn't have any more children, so I was comfortable letting him believe you were his child. He realized that you might be my child, but we agreed to let him take most of the responsibility for you. In fact, I had written the same letter to you in case I was to die first. Then the situation would be reversed. But when Walter died, I told Cedric to destroy my letter because we thought it was better that way. Walter died thinking that you were most likely his child. He died believing that he did the best he could for you."

"I don't know how to take this. Each time I think I had the truth, something else happens and all of what I knew changed. Now what? Whose child am I?"

"You can both take a DNA test. You can find out the truth now." said Ted.

"It's up to you now, Sophie. If you want to find out, we can get to the truth." said Theo.

"I can't think right now." said Sophie. "This is all incredible. I don't know what to believe anymore. Everyone lied to me. My parents, Cedric, Walter, and now you! I have to get out of here. I'll call a cab and go back home."

"Please Sophie. Calm down. I know this is hard for you to understand. Walter and I did the best that we could under the circumstances. We were young, we were in a horrible war, times were different then. We couldn't take care of a baby. We wanted the best for you. We only wanted to give you a good home and your parents were the best. They loved you."

"Will you stop saying that! Everybody tells me that. I know they were wonderful people, but to lie to me like that. That is unacceptable."

"They did not tell you because that was how we arranged it, so don't blame them. You might never have found out if you hadn't found those documents in the attic. Walter, Cedric and I debated about telling you anything. We thought it might be best if you didn't know any of this, especially since we weren't sure which one of us was your father. It just complicated matters, so we decided not to tell you. We couldn't predict the future, that it would have to come out in the end."

Ted weighed in on the situation. "It's strange how one small decision can alter the future."

Theo and Sophie turned to him. "What do you mean?"

"Think about it." said Ted. "What if you and Walter never went to the village where the train was bombed? You would never have found out about her. Sophie would have remained with the Ducros family and would have never known any of this. That's not the only 'What If.' What if no one survived the train? You would not even be here. In fact, if it weren't for a war started by one crazy German, much of life would be different today. Think about it. How many children were born of that war? How many children of American soldiers and French women, or of German soldiers and French women, and so on and so on, all because of the war."

"Since when did you become so philosophical?" asked Theo.

"Hey! I'm only trying to help out my sister."

Sophie looked at him scornfully. "I'm not your sister."

"Well I got you thinking, didn't I? You seemed to have calmed down somewhat."

"I think we need to sleep on this." said Theo. "I'm very tired. Sophie would you please reconsider staying the night? I am really sorry that you have been hurt. I'd like to talk to you more tomorrow. Please stay."

"I guess it wouldn't hurt to stay the night

since it is so late." Sophie replied.

"Ted." Theo said. "Remember you agreed not to talk to your mother. I will decide what to tell her, if I want to tell her, and when."

"I will keep my word. But I want to know more tomorrow."

Ted walked Sophie to the guest house. She was too tired to talk to Ted but he asked her if she was hungry since they missed dinner. She said no. Ted told her that he would bring her breakfast in the morning.

Sophie tried to sleep, but her mind was racing. She had accepted the fact that Walter was her father, and now she must deal with a different truth. *Should I take the DNA test and find out once and for all who my father really is? That would mean that Hélène and not Yvette might be my mother. Should I leave it as it is? What if Theo or Ted insists that I take it? I will not have them run my life anymore. I will take the test if and when I am ready. They can't force me to do it.*

Sophie was awakened by a knock on the door. At first she didn't remember where she was, then the memories of last night came flooding back. Ted brought her something to eat. "Time to get up, sis." he remarked.

"Shut up, Ted. I don't know if I am your sister, and I am not sure if I want to be. You don't seem to be taking this seriously."

"As my father said, I don't have the right to be judgmental. My life hasn't been all that virtuous. I am curious though. He never talked much about his time in the war and I always wondered what he did there. Give the man a break. You couldn't possibly understand what it is like for soldiers away from home fighting for peace and freedom and all that."

"And you couldn't possibly understand what it is like to find out that your whole life was nothing like you thought it was. That your parents are not your parents, then who you found out was your real father may not be after all, that all those people kept secrets from you all your life, that where I am today was all manipulated, that my real mother was French who was killed in the war, and I never got the opportunity to know my biological parents, whoever they might be."

Ted mimicked playing a violin. "Oh you poor thing. Such a hard life."

Sophie had to laugh at Ted. "Ok. You might not be such a bad brother after all."

"Lets go back to the house. My father is up and anxious to see you."

"Mother left early to go shopping, so we can talk freely." said Theo. "I hope you are feeling better this morning, Sophie. Again I want to apologize for everything. Please think about what the situation was like then. Walter and I were young and foolish before the war. We were careless when we started flying. When the war started we thought what a exciting experience it would be to go fly around and bomb the Germans. It wasn't until we were shot down and spent time on the ground with the Resistance that we got a taste of what was really happening. We learned so much from them, especially about what it means to believe in something so much that you would give your life for it. Yvette and Hélène and all the other women should not have had to do the things they did. Wars were supposed to be fought by men. What the Germans did was beyond cruel and inhuman. We wanted to do whatever we could to help the Resistance, but were limited by our responsibilities. When we were rescued from France, we didn't want to go, but had no choice. After Jean-Paul and the others were killed, that was when we saw the real horrors of what a war does to friends and family. We saw the worst of humanity and the best of it. Yvette, Hélène, Cécile and Raymond kept up the fight even through the suffering of their losses. We wanted so much to take Yvette and Hélène here to America and give them a good life. Learning that they had died, we were overwhelmed with grief and guilt. Finding you was a godsend, but we had both lost our loves and one of us lost a child. We knew about the St. Pierre's because they were distant cousins we kept in touch with, and knew that they wanted a child, so the best solution was to have them adopt you. We always wanted to be part of your life, but after we saw how good you were being taken care of and how much they loved you, we didn't want to change anything by interfering. So we helped them financially and watched you from afar."

"Those visits to New York and Chicago were to meet with you and Walter? I remembered Cedric's office in Chicago. I remembered him too as I was afraid of him with his scar when I was little. Then as I got older, I didn't go to the offices. My mother took me sightseeing while my father met with you both."

"Yes Sophie. As you got older, you might have wondered what the meetings were all about, so we didn't want you to hear what we were discussing. After your father met with us, we would go to the museums and watch you with your mother. Sometimes when they would take you to restaurants, we would be at a nearby table. Of course, your parents knew that we were watching you."

"How intriguing." said Ted. "You had this whole other life that we knew nothing about. Sneaking around and everything."

"We weren't sneaking around. The St. Pierres encouraged us to see you, Sophie. They wanted us to know you. They asked numerous times for permission to tell you the truth. But we always put them off saying that someday we would. But that day never came. Let me ask you, do you think it would have made any difference? Do you think your life would have been much different if you knew long ago who you really were?"

"I can't answer that. I don't know. Would I have begun working for *The WorldView* if I knew the job was offered because my father owned it? I can't say."

"I don't think your life would have been much different," said Ted, "but I bet ours would have been. Walter's life and yours might have turned out differently if mother and Walter's wife knew about Sophie."

"No. I think they would have accepted it." said Theo. "It was mostly because of our parents that we kept the secret for so long. Having a child out of wedlock was not acceptable then. So we kept it a secret because we didn't think they would understand. Looking back, maybe we made a mistake, maybe they would have accepted it. But then the St. Pierres would not have had the opportunity to have you. They would have been the biggest losers."

"This is all too much philosophizing. Too many 'What If's.' It is what it is. The question now is what to do next? Will you tell mother? Sophie, will you take the DNA test?"

"As far as your mother is concerned, I will consider telling her. Maybe it will depend on what a DNA test shows. If you are Walter's child, then there is no reason to say anything to your mother."

"Oh, so you are putting this burden on my shoulders?" said Sophie. "I don't know what I want to do."

"Don't take the test Sophie." said Ted. "Let my father wonder about you for the rest of his life. I think that would be a good punishment for keeping you a secret for so long."

"All these years I let myself believe that you are Walter's daughter. If you don't want to take the test, I don't blame you. I will continue to think of you as his daughter." Said Theo.

"If I am not your brother, we are still family. Remember Dad and Walter were cousins, so you are part of our family anyway."

"Yes, I guess I am family. I should thank you, Theo and Walter for supporting my parents and helping me with my education and career. This is not the time for regrets anymore. But I do need to go back home. I'm sorry I can't stay. I need time alone to decide how I feel about all this and what to do about it." Sophie said. "Would you call me a cab so I can take the train back?"

"I'll drive you back." said Ted.

"No, I don't feel like spending the next few hours in a car with you. I really want to be by myself."

"Take my car." Said Theo. "You can drive back to Chicago and leave it anywhere. I'll find it later."

"I still would like to publish your work." said Ted. "I think it would do well and you should get the stories out about the war."

"Yes, I think it's time for the stories of the Resistance should be told. I'll contact you when I'm ready."

"Mother will wonder why you left so quickly," said Ted.

"Tell her something came up. Tell her I had an emergency. Tell her anything you want, and thank her for her hospitality."

Theo apologized again for the way he and Walter handled the situation. "You are welcome here anytime you want to visit. I won't hold you to take the DNA test. I would still like to be involved in your life. I've always loved you too."

Sophie told Theo she was sorry to intrude on his family, but it was really his fault. He was genuinely sorry that it all came out the way it did. Ted tried to insist on taking her back but Theo intervened. He told Ted to leave her be as she has a lot to think about. Ted answered, "So do we."

EPILOGUE

Sophie and Tessa were reminiscing over a glass of fine French wine that Sophie brought back from her last trip to France. It had been a while since she let Ted's company, Griffin Publishing Company publish her book and documentary. Sophie wanted to give a copy of the book to the people that she had interviewed as a thank you for letting her tell their stories. During her visit to France she visited Dominique's family again. She told Dominique about her new dilemma, that either Walter or Theo could be her father, and that meant her mother might be Hélène instead of Yvette.

"Well Sophie, I don't remember what Walter and Theo discussed when they were here. My English was not so good then. But they did ask for the descriptions of the women. No one was able to tell them much as the women were too badly burned. I'm sorry that doesn't help you." said Dominique.

"I could take the DNA test and find out for sure, but I don't know if I want to do it."

"Why not?" asked Dominique.

"I like to think of Walter and Yvette as my parents since they let me believe that for so long, and because Walter could not have any other children after his injuries. But then if Theo and Hélène are my parents I'd have Theo's family as my family now. It would be like having the best of both of them. Theo has children and grandchildren. They are good people. I met them all at events and parties that the company had. I was introduced to the family, but only Theo and his son Ted know about me. Theo didn't tell his wife about his affair with Hélène. If I take the test, it would finalize things and I don't think I am ready to do that yet."

"Even if you do not want to find out for sure, you already know that you have a French mother, and that Walter and Theo have British heritage. You were born here in France and adopted and raised in America. That means you are a good combination of nationalities."

"Yes, that's a good feeling." said Sophie.

Then Sophie visited Cécile and Raymond. Raymond was enjoying renewed fame as he was singing again. Since Sophie had added stories about them and the Resistance group they were part of, people wanted to hear Raymond's stories and songs. Cécile told Sophie that more young people were becoming interested in their old war stories and Raymond seemed more than willing to talk to them about the war.

"After you visited us," said Cécile, "Raymond had been depressed for so long that I think you helped him realize it was time to stop being sad for what might have been, and begin living for the present. Honoring our friends with his songs has become a new goal for him. We thank you for helping us and telling our story in your book."

"I'm glad to have been a help. There is so much about wars that people don't realize how much it affects individuals and their families. Maybe understanding this will cause people to think about other solutions to solve world problems besides fighting with each other."

"I wonder if society will ever learn that wars can't solve every problem."

"I also want to thank you for telling me stories about Yvette and Hélène. I wish there was some family of theirs that I could connect with. That might have helped me make a decision to take the DNA test."

"What matters is that they both gave their lives for our country. They were both brave women. I'm just happy that you are the child of one of them, and that, in a way, both of them will live on in you."

Sophie then contacted Cedric to tell him that she would accept the inheritance. She added a stipulation that the interest in her shares of the stock would be donated to two charities, Wounded Warriors and Battered Women's Clinics. Sophie would visit the mansion Walter owned in upstate New York and decide later what to do with it. She wanted to go through Walter's things and see if she could find the letters from Yvette hoping that might help her with a decision.

Sophie returned to New Orleans for a big class reunion. She and Tessa were sitting in Sophie's kitchen the night before the reunion enjoying the French wine.

"It's hard to believe all the things we went through." said Tessa. "When we graduated the only plans we had were to get married and bake cookies for our children."

Sophie laughed. "I wonder where we would be if we made different decisions then. That's the old What-If game. What if I had married Wayne and never accepted the job at *The WorldView*. Would I have been happily married with children and never thought about a career?"

"And what if I wasn't so naïve and in a hurry to get married thinking Geoff was going to be a wonderful husband since he wanted to be a doctor. I thought what a great life that was going to be."

"Did we make choices because we were meant to be where we are today? Could we have changed our fate with one small decision long ago?" wondered Sophie.

"You mean, is it destiny that brought us here? Who knows. I think at this point it doesn't really matter. It is what it is, as they say. We can't change the past, so why worry about what might have been."

"At this point in my life, I wonder what I am leaving behind, what will my legacy be? You have your children and grandchildren to remember you by. But I have nothing." said Sophie.

"That's not true." said Tessa. "You have your work, your books and photographs. Those are your legacy, your children, so to speak. Books and photographs last a long time, probably longer than my grandchildren and great grandchildren will remember me."

"What is next for us? I wonder." said Sophie.

"I don't know, but I plan on continuing to work for the clinics. I enjoy what I am doing and I think I am making a difference in some women's lives."

"I am at another crossroad, I think. I don't have any idea about what to do next. Should I write another book? Should I travel to places I haven't been yet? Should I stay here a while?" Sophie pondered. "It seems that we have traded places. You are now enjoying a career traveling around the country to the new clinics, and I think I just want to stay home for a while and visit my city, see what changes have happened over the years, and see what happens next."

"What's next is the reunion tomorrow." answered Tessa. "There are people we haven't seen since the last reunion years ago. Just enjoy that and see what our old friends are up to."

"That will be fun to catch up on their lives. I wonder how much different they are."

"Different? I'll tell you one life that is different. Did you know that Wayne is divorced?"

"No. I haven't heard that. What happened?" asked Sophie.

"He found out that his wife had been having an affair with her boss. It had been going on for a long time so he was pretty upset about it. They recently divorced but he got over it quickly. I think he never got over you. I think he always loved you."

"Oh? I don't know. People get on with their lives and the past is long forgotten."

Sophie arrived at the reunion late. She met with friends who congratulated her for her accomplishments as she also complimented them on their achievements. She joined Tessa at the bar who was there with a new friend she made from work. Sophie and Tessa were looking out at the Crescent City Connection Bridge that crossed the Mississippi River admiring the view while waiting for their drinks. Suddenly Tessa looked up behind Sophie as Sophie felt a hand on her shoulder.

"Hello Sophie."

Sophie turned around and looked up at a distinguished grey haired man.

"Hello Wayne."

AUTHOR'S NOTE

It was a time when the world witnessed the most infamous, evil and dangerous of men, and the most courageous and heroic. World War II brought out the evils of Hitler, Mussolini, Stalin and Hirohito all working together to gain world domination, then Stalin changing sides as Hitler turned against him by invading Russia. On opposite sides of the world, powerful armies could have defeated America and the Allies. But heroes such as Roosevelt, Truman, Eisenhower, Patton, Churchill, MacArthur, and millions of civilians who joined the armed forces, combined with the French Resistance civilians who fought on their own or with groups helped to defeat the enemy, win the war, and gain their freedom back. Never before have so many young people joined forces individually and as groups to fight for their rights and their country. This, the deadliest of wars, claimed more civilians than military with estimates of up to a total of 80 million people killed.

This is a work of fiction. However much research was done to follow a timeline of events for it to be historical. I did extensive research of the French Resistance members of that time. It turned out to be the most fascinating reading I have done to date. There are many non-fiction books written about the Resistance by the actual members themselves, by researchers who interviewed them, by other authors who wrote close to the time period while the memories were fresh, and some much later. Many fiction books were also written by numerous authors, some living in the time and place of the war. The most notable is *Silence of the Sea,* by Vercors, a pseudonym for Jean Bruller, living in France at the time.

There are also numerous websites that have recently been created since online research has exploded. Some researchers are now finding forgotten documents such as the underground newspapers that were important to the Resistance Movement. These documents are being copied in many forms such as PDF files and posted on the internet for posterity to be able to read them in their original form. Other web sites include long forgotten photographs from the war.

Documentaries are being produced for television stations which show films taken by photographers caught up in the fighting.

Much of the interest in the war came about because of the 70th anniversary in 2015 of the end of the war.

No fictional spy story or thriller is better than the true story of the Resistance Fighters in France during World War II. There was not just one or two or ten individuals doing heroic acts as seen in a good spy movie, but tens of thousands of French civilians. They planned activities on their own, sometimes taking orders from others, but many times working alone with better results than an army because they did what they felt needed to be done on their own terms when and where it was needed. These were ordinary people from all walks of life working together, people who never expected to have to turn their lives around to become freedom fighters.

All the elements that make up a great thriller; espionage, counterespionage, secret codes, code names, executions, treachery, betrayals, safe houses, escape routes, heroes, villains, sex, sleeping with the enemy, secret parachute drop zones, guerrilla warfare, daring and dangerous prison breakouts, and more can be found in the real stories of these patriotic heroes of wartime and war torn France. It is truly a wonder that with all the events that occurred, with loyalties constantly changing, not knowing who to trust from one day to the next, collaborations with the Germans, French loyalties to either General de Gaulle or General Giraud, that things actually fell into place against all odds, and France was finally liberated, and the Allies won the war. The French people believed in their freedoms and fought bravely, too many dying for their country. Their true life stories should be on everyone's reading list.

One of the best nonfiction books written about this period is *Soldiers of the Night,* by David Schoenbrun, who was there as a war correspondent and witnessed first hand many of the events of WWII. As a correspondent, he had access to and met with most of the main players of the French and Allies. The book was published in 1980 and was available on Amazon at the time of this writing.

Following is a list of the resources and books I used as research for this story. It is certainly an incomplete list, but is a beginning for anyone who wants to read a more comprehensive account of the Resistance members and their fight for freedom.

Fiction:
Brown, James and Lawrence Stokes. (2002), *Silence of the Sea/Le Silence de la Mer: A Novel of French*

Resistance during the Second World War by 'Vercors" (Bloomsbury Academic).

Faulks, Sebastian. (1993), *Birdsong: A Novel of Love and War* (Vintage)

Monsarrat, Nicholas. (1951), *The Cruel Sea* (Burford Books, Inc.).

Rutherfurd, Edward. (2013), *Paris* (Random House).

Non-fiction:

Aubrac, Lucie. (1994), *Outwitting the Gestapo* (Knickerbocker Press).

Cobb, Matthew. (2009), *The Resistance: The French Fight Against the Nazis* (Pocket Books).

Collins, Larry and Dominique Lapierre. (2000), *Is Paris Burning?* é(Castle Books).

Fourcade, Marie-Madeline. (1974), *Noah's Ark* (Ballantine Books).

Moorehead, Caroline. (2011), *A Train in Winter* (HarperCollins).

Schoenbrun, David. (1980), *Soldiers of the Night* (Meridian).

Vinen, Richard. (2006), *The Unfree French* (Yale University Press).

Weitz, Margaret Collins. (1995), *Sisters in the Resistance: How Women Fought to Free France, 1940-1945* (John Wiley & Sons, Inc.).

Multimedia:

The History Channel has shown many documentaries about the World Wars. A search on their website will list these, when they will be shown, and how they can be purchased.

PhotosNormandie on Flicker has thousands of original photographs catalogued in albums by topics and areas.

Made in the USA
San Bernardino, CA
20 October 2015